THE BOOKS
OF ANGUISH
(Volume 3)

BY THE SAME AUTHOR

Ortog (translated by Brian Stableford)
The Improbables/The 32nd of July (translated by Michael Shreve)
Black Sheep/The Children of History (translated by Michael Shreve)
Blood Light/A Shroud of Mist (The Books of Anguish 1) (translated by Sheryl Curtis)
Mortefontaine/The Threshold of the Void (The Books of Anguish 2) (translated by Sheryl Curtis)

THE BOOKS
OF ANGUISH
(Volume 3)
The Shores of Night
The Village of Lepers

by
Kurt Steiner

translated by
Sheryl Curtis

A Black Coat Press Book

Acknowledgements: Thanks to Julien Forest, Jean-Luc Rivera and Philippe Ward.

Visit our website at www.blackcoatpress.com

TABLE OF CONTENTS

KURT STEINER

LES RIVAGES DE LA NUIT

M. Gourdon

ANGOISSE

Éditions
"FLEUVE NOIR"

Introduction

In 1954, I read the very first title published in the *"Angoisse"* imprint, *Le Cimetière de la Peur* by Donald Wandrei,[1] with great interest, and it encouraged me to contribute to that imprint. From that point on, I felt able to write horror stories drawing on Gothic themes, such as ghosts, vampires, zombies, curses, etc. *The Sound of Silence* was my first contribution, number 13 in the series... Some might see a special meaning there... It remains one of my favorite novels.

The *fantastique* as a literary genre really took form in the 19th century. There had been fantastical works before, but the genre itself became more clearly structured during the 19th century. It could be considered as a natural continuation of various medieval works of fantasy whose themes were mostly about Love and Death, such as *Tristan and Isolde*. These also relied on themes such as witchcraft, magic spells, the Devil, like in the fairy tales. The genre underwent some profound changes during the 19th century due to the evolution of occultism, black magic, as well as various odd medical experiments conducted by people like Franz Mesmer. This new research gave the *fantastique* a more metaphysical grounding.

When writing spontaneously as I do – something required when producing a series of popular novels – it is necessary to first settle on an outline which can give maximum consistency to the rest of the work. An ex-

---

[1] *The Web of Easter Island, Arkham House, 1948*

tremely fast writing method will favor both lyricism and the use of colorful images. On the other hand, a certain form of poetry always remains inseparable from classic fantasy.

These styles were reconciled during the 19th century in popular works that were rich in action and twists and from which the *fantastique* was not excluded. Any such works can be crafted in several ways. Two of these, diametrically opposed, can be equally effective. First, there is what I call the "static" fantasy. Take for example *Blood Light:* all he action takes place inside a castle. In *Les Dents Froides*, my characters stay for twenty-four hours on the wreck of a ship. In either case, the books rely entirely on an atmospheric *fantastique.*

Alternatively, one can also craft a novel based on pure action, a series of supernatural events which will play a predominant role and serve as driving elements for the action. *A Shroud of Mist* or *Mortefontaine* fall in that category.

In the end, I see the *fantastique* as a "shield, a means of defense against the monotony of daily life and one of the few avenues of escape that our modern-day life offers. It is, if you like, a shield similar to that which can be caused by an attack of fever during an infectious disease.

The *fantastique* thus becomes truly therapeutic. It can prove beneficial, but if the transition into the *fantastique* exceeds certain limits, overwhelming reason, then we should fight it in the same way we fight a lasting fever.

Kurt Steiner
1970

THE SHORES OF NIGHT

FLETCHER CRAWSON'S ACCOUNT

CHAPTER I

Behind the tall windows, January shook its snowy hair. On the small square I looked down on, spindly trees, weighed down by icy cotton, trembled in their wrought iron tree guards shining with frost. In the fountain basins, a few solitary plates of ice served as a reminder of the good old days of triumphant water sprays. The streetlights, standing in a line, with their large, blinding heads perched ridiculously at the top of long slender stems, cast a cruder, somewhat more glacial gaze over this muddy whiteness here and there.

I looked away from this barely real landscape, separated from me by a thin sheet of glass and glanced around the calm warm universe of the library. The tall, polished shelves, with their millions of pages crammed in a motionless journey, joined the long oak tables to create a strange world of horizontal and vertical lines under the banker's lamps with their green shades where odd puppets maintained an unsettling stillness, broken only, from time to time, by the rustling of a page being turned.

A few meters away, a small, shriveled old woman with a graying bun on the top of her skull, was peering through spectacles from another century at the violently colored cover of an issue of the "Petit Journal" depicting the fire at the Bazar de la Charité.

Despite the distance, I was able to see the terrible realism the designer had not feared to use when portraying the cadavers that had been blackened and scorched by the fire, lying in the midst of collapsed beams.

What depths of repressed sadism lay in the heart of this peaceful looking grandmother for her to sneak into the library, at night, to consult the collection of these outdated publications in which each issue was more chilling than the last?

Farther off, to my right, a man sitting with his back to me was leaning against a table arranged parallel to mine. His black jacket, shiny with wear, outlined the narrowness of his shoulders and, with his two arms crossed in front of him and resting on the piece of oak furniture, he looked like one of those large birds of prey with its long, bald skull sitting on top of a massive body and folded wings. Other readers were seated here and there in the large room but they were too far away from me for me to be able to provide a precise description.

I returned to the ancient document I had decided to read. The overwhelming allegorical presumption of the text had managed to finally make me look away, to observe the universe of reality for a few minutes.

I looked back at the pages, yellowed over time, that had been difficult to locate in the closed stacks. I was only able to consult it as a result of the archivist's friendship. It was an extraordinarily complex drama in which each character embodied a specific human vice or virtue. I had reached a passage in which strangeness overwhelmed the fastidious and emphatic character just when a new individual, unknown up to that point, appeared to take charge of the situation. I started to read the following sentence:

"The castle seemed to be completely buried under the thick snow know only to Rhenish winters and, through the tall window in the parlor, the margrave observed the countryside where plague and famine reigned, hidden under the lintel of January. A knock at the door.

"Come in," said the master, thinking that one of the servants was coming for orders.

But, as the door opened, it revealed a tall stranger, looking pitiful in tattered black clothing.

"What's this?" shouted the margrave. "Who are you and how did you manage to get in here without my people coming to warn me?"

"My apologies," said the man. "My name is Ulrich von Heiligenshtadt and I share your blood..."

As I finished reading that sentence, I looked up, jumping. The man in black that I had observed sitting motionless at the other table had stood up without making a sound and was now standing in front of me, leaning slightly forward.

"I beg your pardon, for interrupting your reading," he said. "I'm taking notes about an important matter and I find I've suddenly run out of materials. Would you have a little ink in your pen or could you loan ma a mechanical pencil?"

Once standing, the man seemed very tall and very thin. His black clothing shone with wear. He spoke with a pronounced German accent.

At the time, I did not know quite what to do. I was torn between the obligation to be of service to him and the infinitely strange sensation caused by the simultaneity, the superposition of a living person with the character who had spoken the sentence I had just been reading. I was obliged to note, moreover, that the two characters, the real one and the fictional one, were similar in some strange manner, and that there was some sort of equivalence, in the framework and the period, that could not escape my notice.

I stared at him dumbfounded and I must have looked like a simpleton or a man caught up in some stupid act to him. I recovered and finally muttered some indistinct excuse.

"I'm sorry," I said. "I have nothing of the kind on me. I suggest you ask the librarian who will certainly be pleased to give you the items you need."

I thought the man would head immediately to the archivist's office but he did nothing of the sort. He placed both of his hands on my table, bent slightly and remained there, motionless, for a moment. His face was just above the green lampshade and I felt slightly uncomfortable when I saw his face, in the dim light, cut into geometric shapes by the unusual and deathly light. That, combined with the surprising coincidence that connected him to the character in the book made me hunker down against the back of my chair, seeking comfort. In vain.

He glanced at the open book lying in front of me and something akin to irony shone in his deeply sunken eyes.

"Curious…" he said. "A curious document. Where did you manage to find it?"

He straightened up and continued, "I cannot continue my boring conversation with you without introducing myself to you."

He remained silent for a moment, while I leisurely savored the fear of what was to come.

"My name is Ulrich von Heiligenshtadt," he said.

Then the man left, striding silently. I watched him walk away, dumbfounded. When he disappeared into the archivist's office, I recovered from my torpor and feverishly read the extraordinary paragraph again. But, although I ran my eyes over the two pages first quickly then more slowly, re-reading certain fragments I had already gone over, and even moving onto what I had not read as yet, I found no mention anywhere of the mysterious Ulrich, although the other characters were still present.

I abandoned my reading with the feeling that something incomprehensible and unusual had erupted into the natural order of things and that the peaceful library was the theater for an unprecedented event. With my mind filled with all sorts of vague suppositions, I looked at the door to the archivist's office for a long time, the door which the stranger had walked through just a few moments earlier.

The landscape outside, petrified in the glacial night, had not changed at all. Neither had the silent and comfortable atmosphere in the library. Either there was something unsettling about the matter or I had to question my sanity. I could not bear the eruption of the impossible in such banal circumstances and, overwhelmed by a sudden need for action, I suddenly stood up.

I stood there, undecided, for a few seconds, looking from the office door, to the book, then back to the door. I finally made up my mind and headed hesitantly in the direction of the office. I knocked on the oak door.

"Come in," said a voice inside.

I pushed the door. In the room littered with papers and books, the archivist welcomed me with a questioning smile. He was alone.

"I... I..." I stammered. "Didn't you..." I stopped short.

"Do you want another book, Mr. Crawson? The man asked kindly.

"It's that... "I stammered again, dumbfounded, looking at the walls without discovering a door other than the one I had come in through. "I thought someone had come to visit you."

The archivist looked somewhat surprised.

"Visit me!" he said "Did you think you would find me here with a cup of tea in hand, discussing glorious military memories?

He smiled with the satisfied air of someone who was enjoying his own joke. I did not smile back and the expression on my face must have surprised him since he walked over to me, frowning, observing me closely.

"Explain yourself," he added. "I have no idea what you're going on about."

I dug automatically through my pants pocket and pulled out a handkerchief, which I wiped over my forehead where perspiration was starting to bead.

"Excuse me, Mr. Flanders," I said, patting the damp palms of my hands with the handkerchief. "I could have sworn that a man, a reader, had come in here to ask you for some ink. I... I wonder if I might have fallen asleep for a few seconds and dreamed it all."

He continued to stare at me and replied, in a determined tone, "No doubt, sir... no doubt at all."

He waved his hand at me.

"You know… dreams are extremely fleeting things. You doze for a moment and a dream comes, in a flash, fitting in between you and reality, and your mind does not recognize it as a dream. These things happen, Mr. Crawson, these things happen…"

I stepped back, dumbfounded.

"That's likely," I murmured. "Yet I remember the man perfectly, his tortured features, his black clothing, even his name."

"His name!" exclaimed the archivist. "Now that's unusual! People don't usually remember names that they hear, that they believe they hear in dreams!"

"Oh!" I exclaimed. "Such an unusual name, it comes as no surprise that I remember it."

"Yes." said Flanders. "And that name would be?"

"German. It sounded German or Austrian: Ulrich von Heiligenshtadt."

Flanders suddenly took two steps back.

"You said Heiligenshtadt?" he said, his voice cracking.

"Yes," I replied. And that's what seemed so strange to me. I had just read that same name in the book you loaned me."

"Of course," said Flanders. "That's the name of the principal character in *Tragic Philosophies* by Clara Conway, that curious work written by a medium in the first half of the 18th century. Obviously, you know that work since you asked me for it."

I stiffened. Sweat was starting to bead on my forehead.

"Well…" I said. "Come and take a look at that book. I challenge you to find anyone named Ulrich. I thought I had read that name myself but after the man spoke to me or, if you prefer, after my dream, I could find no reference in *Tragic Philosophies* to Heiligenshtadt."

Flanders shrugged.

"Let's go," he said. "You left the book on your table? Go ahead of me. We'll clear this up."

When we got to the table where I had spent several hours, I was almost relieved to see the book open under the lamp. What would I have done if it had disappeared? How would I have explained to Flanders the extravagant ideas running around in my head? But *Tragic Philosophies* was still there, motionless and reassuring.

Flanders picked the book up greedily, read a few lines, turned a few pages, read a paragraph, went back a few pages, re-read half a page feverishly, flipped through to the end, read again. He pushed it aside, stood up, looking at me. The green light of the lamp emphasized the paleness of his face.

"Crawson," he said, in a hesitant tone. "I'm missing something here. I admit that I can't find the name of the main character either. Yet I recall it very strongly. I don't know if we're both hallucinating or if our memories are playing tricks on us. But what's happening is beyond my understanding."

I believe that he made a very small sign of the cross over the book with his finger, but I could not confirm this since his gesture was so furtive.

"What the devil!" I exclaimed. "We have to have seen that name somewhere since we both know it."

The old woman looked up and glanced at us furiously through her spectacles.

"Shh," she said imperiously.

The magazine open in front of her showed a colorful drawing of a guillotine with a bloody head. We both looked at her, indignation mingling with guilt, as she grumbled in a low voice, "Speaking in a library should be forbidden! Particularly in a foreign language!"

We had spoken in English and that seemed to displease her. I must say that she had to feel at a disadvantage since she must have been quite certain we understood her.

Flanders spoke in French, saying "You're right Madam. As the librarian, I should set an example. Come Crawson. We'll speak in my office."

He was already heading in the direction of the door, which had remained open, when I stopped at a window that looked out over the black night. My exclamation made him double back and I pointed, my finger trembling, at something in the middle of the square. He looked in the direction I was indicating.

"Well, well," he said "Now that's extraordinary!"

"What's extraordinary?" I shouted. "Do you see that tall man, dressed in black, sitting on the edge of the fountain? Well, that's the man who spoke to me. He's the one I saw go into your office... That's Heiligenshtadt and he seems to have escaped from the book!"

Flanders had placed his face against the window and was staring avidly at the man who was about 30 meters away, lit clearly enough by a streetlight that we were able to see his silhouette and his large, bald forehead.

As we stood there, petrified, watching, we saw the man raise his head in such a way that, even if we could not see his eyes, we could legitimately presume he was looking at us.

He stood up slowly, walked a few steps in the light, gradually stepped in the shadow of the trees where his outline stood out against the snow and in an uncertain manner, although we both had the same impression at the same time, something frightful happened. It seemed to me that he continued to walk without moving his legs, as his loose-fitting coat flowed like a pair of wings and he rose in heavy flight above the ground. But my terrified sigh of amazement merely echoed Flanders' who looked at me, eyes wide.

"Did you see that?" he said. "He vanished completed, as if sinking into the snow…"

I turned to the archivist, feeling as if the skin of my face were shrinking, as it turned cold and brittle.

"No," I said. "I saw him fly away… like a bat… an immense bat."

Behind us, a pile of paper fell noisily to the floor. The old woman, who was obsessed with catastrophes and executions bent down to pick up a stack of newspapers that had just fallen.

She turned to us and yelped, "It's all your fault… I won't be coming back here. And tomorrow I'll inform the mayor about how the archivist does his job… chatting out loud… in a foreign language."

She threw her library card down furiously and quickly pulled on her ragged, black fur coat. Then she stomped out of the room.

We both stood there, looking back and forth from the door that had closed behind her to the snow-covered square below us.

"Well, well," said Flanders, in a tone filled with fake joviality. "Here I am again, without a job, reduced to going back to my old translations."

We were alone in the vast room that looked even more imposing in the confidential light of the green lamps.

"You know full well that old witch will do nothing and you also know full well that is not what concerns us. What exactly did you see?"

He turned serious again. I felt some suffocating threat thicken around us, emanating from the thousands of books and the deserted room., transforming in the heat that was curiously present, ready to burst into fire.

Flanders placed his hand on my shoulder.

"In a trap..." he said. "Like falling into a trap... completely erased... there... in full light."

I looked at him, shivering despite the intense heat.

"Not at all," I said. "I saw him fly off heavily."

I remained silent. It didn't matter that we had different interpretations. In any case, in our minds, we had both seen a crack through which logic and reason had fled, leaving behind ruin and delusion. Yet, the situation was quite unsettling and I could see by Flanders' attitude that he was most uncomfortable. I refused to grow agitated any further by his dark threats of madness and wished the archivist good evening, adding that I would see him the next morning.

"Have a good night and try not to dream too much..."

But his hand when he shook mine was cold and trembled.

CHAPTER II

When I left the library, the cold gripped me like a giant hand. The snow, which had been falling for several days over Paris, a city I did not know well, transformed things into objects that had been painted or drawn with supernatural precision. I wrapped my thick wool coat tightly around me and pulled my scarf up over my nose. Hat pulled down low, my hands in my gloves, my gloves in my pockets, I started my almost silent trip down the white sidewalk.

After ten steps, I slowed, then stopped. Why shouldn't I go and examine the area around the fountain, the place where, while I was standing in the reading room, I thought I saw the man dressed in black walk about, then disappear? The sidewalk I was walking along ran around the square and I merely had to cross the street and I would find myself in the square where the fountain stood. I looked cautiously right, then left along the almost deserted street since cars are dangerously silent in snowy weather. I finally crossed the street and made my way under the line of streetlights and trees. To my right, about 15 meters from the fountain, just at the edge of the square, I saw something that surprised me, while providing a hint of an explanation: two sets of stairs, standing side by side. The first led down steeply to a metro entrance; the other connected the square to a street above it where the traffic was thicker. A small narrow road ran from the square to this bridge-like structure and I realized that, if the man in black had truly existed, he could have disappeared before our eyes, as Flanders believed, by slipping away through the snow, namely by walking down the stairs to the metro, or by gently flying off, as I had thought, by climbing up the stairs to the small road I found myself standing under. All in all, we could have imagined everything and he could have simply walked down the poorly lit street, that faded into the distance.

Confused, I headed back to the square. Had we really seen something or someone? In any case, the man who had spent a few moments sitting on the edge of the fountain most likely had nothing in common with the absurd invention created by my tired mind, namely the character I had thought was mentioned in the novel although he did not actually exist in that book.

I had dreamed it. And yet, my words had been so convincing they had exercised some sort of power of suggestion over Flanders so strong they had overcome his defenses.

I retraced my steps, somewhat less disturbed than before. But then, one particularly unexpected detail cast doubt over everything. On the almost immaculate layer of snow covering the square, a series of footprints headed from the edge of the fountain in my direction. I was walking parallel to them. Taking care not to muddy them, I had to admit that they started at the edge of the stone fountain, as if the man who had made them had stepped out of the fountain.

Dumbfounded, I stood there for a moment, examining the incomprehensible footprints. Then I walked back along them, heading in the same direction they did.

Another amazing revelation waited for me at the edge of the square: the footprints branched off. One set headed down the stairs to the metro and the others headed up to the overhead street, as if the man who had made them had split into two and taken two separate paths.

No! I could not accept that unreasonable supposition. There must be some sort of trickery and I just knew I had to uncover it.

I returned to the fountain and walked around it. I sighed in relief. Coming from the other side of the square, the same footprints stopped at the edge of the fountain basin at a point diametrically opposite the site where I had seen them head off.

Thus, the man had arranged the entire scene, for who knows whatever reason. He had crossed the basin, walking on the ice from which the wind had cleared the snow and had stepped onto the square as if rising out of the ground. No doubt he had then walked around the square, after taking the stairs that led to the overhead street, had stepped in the same footprints and changed his destination, walking down the stairs to the metro. This explained everything as simply as possible. But after I took a few steps, everything collapsed again.

The footsteps started abruptly about 10 meters from the fountain as if the man had fallen from the sky.

To keep everything as logical as possible, I had to presume that the man in black had retraced his footsteps, and covered the first segments of the prints with snow. And all this crooked scaffolding of quirky hypotheses drew me to the absurd idea of an occult intervention. It was already odd enough that the footprints were almost the only ones on the square and it would be impossible to require explanations they would be incapable of providing. What would Flanders have thought if he had accompanied me on this strange, absurd search! Instinctively, I looked up at the library windows. I was amazed to see two silhouettes there. One was very tall; he seemed to be caught up in a lively discussion and was gesturing wildly. No doubt, the smaller, stockier shape was Flanders. The other could only be the impossible Heiligenshtadt.

I was about to set off when a third silhouette appeared behind the poorly lit windows. I do know what I generally look like. This third silhouette looked so much like me that I stood there, frozen.

My once peaceful session at the library was taking a mindboggling turn. I finally set aside the sudden heaviness in my legs and rushed clumsily to the edge of the sidewalk where I lost my balance and fell violently forward. The fall left me dazed for a good minute and, when I got back to my feet, I noticed that the reading room windows were dark.

I looked up and down the street. About 50 meters away, on my right, a very tall individual was racing down the sidewalk that the library looked down over. To the left, a small man, bundled up against the weather, was walking in the opposite direction.

I was immediately convinced that the two men were Flanders and Heiligenshtadt, but my inability to choose quickly between the two and possibly my fear of following the larger man made me hesitate and I quickly lost sight of them. That left the third shape I had seen in the window. He must have remained inside. All in all, that one was of the most interest to me, given its resemblance to myself.

I crossed the street. The large door to the public monument was not locked. Since there was no concierge, I entered the building easily.

I turned on the light in the lobby and started to climb painfully up the stairs, favoring my injured right knee. The silence here was as thick as the nightly cotton of the snow and the carpet covering the stairs muffled my footsteps so thoroughly, I thought I had grown deaf.

As I climbed the stairs, the malaise that had gripped me when I entered the building intensified degree by degree. By the time I reached the second floor, it had grown into an unbearable anguish. I felt that something unbelievably sinister waited for me in the reading room. I stopped at the closed door. In the back of my mind, I felt surprised that I had managed to get so far without being stopped by a single guard or lock.

I pushed the door. It too was unlocked. The large room was completely dark and I wandered about a few minutes, looking for a light switch. I finally found one and all of the small lamps with their green lampshades turned on at the same time. I started walking along the walls covered with bookshelves, stepping around the tables, which I glanced at, in concern. Everything seemed normal; there was no mystery, and I returned to my starting point without noticing anything alarming. Yet the anxiety that had been tormenting me had not varied a single moment and I was afraid to go into the archivist's office or the closed stacks. Perhaps Flanders had locked both rooms before leaving. Yet, I could not stay there forever. What if some police officer patrolling the street saw lights on in the reading room at such a late hour and came upstairs to ask me what I was doing there? I might be accused of trying to burgle the place and my good faith would most likely not go very far in my defense.

No matter what it cost me, I could not leave the premises without at least glancing into Flanders' office. I walked over to it. The door opened easily. When the light flooded the archive room, I took a step back, my throat constricted by fear. At my feet, a man who looked exactly like me, lay on his back. Thirty or thirty-five years old, hooked nose, auburn hair... identical beige tweed clothing, suede shoes, brown gabardine shirt and ivory tie. His blue eyes were wide open and seemed to be staring in horror at a corner of the ceiling. I bent down and placed my hand on his chest, under his jacket... His heart was not beating. No sign of injury.

The terror that washed over me was so intense I remained kneeling on the floor for a long time, incapable of doing anything at all. The quiet warmth of the office, with its stacks of books provided an unreal, banal backdrop for my discovery of my own cadaver.

I stood up slowly, and I must have looked terrified as I backed out of the office.

My retreat down the silent, deserted, brightly lit staircase is burned in my memory like a moment from someone else's life. Before leaving, I turned off all the lights in the office and the reading room. I even turned off the lights in the hall and the staircase, out of a desire for tranquility and correctness, both of which seemed out of place at such a time.

When I found myself back on the white sidewalk, a passerby studied my face, then turned away and walked off. I thought to myself that he would step forward as a witness in the criminal case that would break the next morning. The police would be chasing after me for a crime I had perpetrated against myself, a crime that could not be a suicide. They would see me as a Fletcher Crawson look-alike and I would be accused of murdering him to steal his identity. And if my fingerprints proved I was the real Crawson, I would be accused of killing my double for some reason they would have no problem inventing. And if, finally, the cadaver's fingerprints were the same as mine, that would no doubt create an extraordinary problem for the courts, but I would still be accused of murder because I was still alive. Of course, all they would have against me would be presumptions based on the testimony of the passerby, but it is a well-known fact that, when faced with the impossibility of proving guilt, although guilt is probable or seems so, any jury would render a verdict of uncertainty, that would still earn me 15 to 20 years in prison.

I stood there, motionless, on the sidewalk, in front of the library, and the thoughts that swirled in my mind so rapidly, like lightning, made me shiver as much as the cold did. I watched the potential witness as he walked on with uneven footing, without turning back, and suddenly, a powerful desire to kill him overwhelmed me. If I let that man live, I would have to live a miserable life in hiding until the police came to drag me off to prison. If I managed to make him disappear, certain that I would not be seen, no one would come to accuse me, for the simple reason that everyone would think I was dead. In the one case, my existence would be aborted in the depths of a prison cell; in the other, I would start a new life, with a new identity. As for my desire to kill, I had never felt anything like it before. In the past, I would have calmly examined that sudden passionate hatred, as if from outside myself, yet now I discovered a sinister personality within myself, one I accepted without questioning, because I had become that and nothing else.

I decided to chase after the man. The wind had come up, making an impalpable, icy dust swirl above the ground, dust made of white sand that had strangely lost its way in the black city, along the shores of night. I peered somberly through the deserted night looking into the distance, as the man, dwarfed by distance, re-appeared under one street light after another. His comical gait, no doubt caused by patches of ice here and there, made him look like he was hopping. When I started walking, quickly yet carefully, my throat tightened. I was heading out of the world of ghosts and into that of assassins.

The heavy chimes of a distant church bell spread the rosary of their hopeless appeals over the pale city and I recall that, at that very moment, I found something threatening in the funereal color of the nocturnal carillon that evoked a strangely clandestine death knell like the one chimed by a terrified priest in the depths of a city decimated by an epidemic.

The man was still a great distance from me. I picked up my pace, torn between the desire to catch up with him as quickly as possible and the fear that I would reveal my presence through my awkward efforts to trail after him. On that wide, empty, terribly brightly lit avenue, I felt as helpless as if I had been caught in the worst nightmare. The scrunch of each footstep I took in the snow told me I was going to kill a man, the pounding in my temples accused me of being a murderer and the mortal chiming in the distance proclaimed an imminent death… Everything proved to me I did not have what it took to be a murderer amplifying my fear that my bloody project would fail.

Yet the distance between us was growing smaller second by second. The chiming stopped, leaving me along to face my deed. Other fears washed over me. What if the prey was stronger than the hunter? Don't be silly! I had seen the man when he walked past me. He was thin, his back was hunched, his face was already old. Above all, it was essential that no one witness my attack. He was now about 50 meters from me and I was starting to undo my tie, as I continued to walk. I wrapped one end around each hand, creating a treacherous and silent weapon. My heart was beating so loudly and I was so extremely nervous, that I feared I would reveal my presence to my future victim. With all my might, I pushed aside the wave of horror I had been struggling with so I could clearly attain the machine-like detachment I required to fulfill my project. I must have turned into another man since I managed to do so without catching my victim's attention.

I had decided to get close enough to the man that I could leap on him in one stride, throw him to the ground, and wrap the improvised garrote I held in my hands around his neck. It would take me less than a minute to strangle him fully, and after doing that I would then run off down some side street where my trail would be quickly lost.

I was no more than 20 meters behind the man and was already gathering my strength for my final attack when the avenue, which had been deserted up to that point, started to come alive. Misfortune was following and could well save the one who would be my downfall. At the end of the road, some theatre must have just finished its show, spitting out the theater-goers. Groups of two or three people were walking down the sidewalk in my direction, about 100 meters away, and all too quickly a larger group reached the sidewalk I was on. I had to hide my tie in my coat pocket and continue trailing after the man until we reached some place with far fewer potential witness. Fortunately, the man continued to walk at a steady pace, paying no attention to what was going on behind him. Nothing in his attitude seemed to indicate that he was getting close to his home.

Ten meters ahead of me, the man continued to walk, running headlong into an army of people bundled up against the snow and the night who looked, following their fleeting escape through the silver screen, much like the crazy characters in James Ensor's paintings.

After increasing in density, the unfortunate theatergoers grew rarer and rarer, with only a few latecomers dragging their heels. But a new obstacle appeared, since we had now reached the theater from which they had billowed, and we were walking so quickly that we would soon run into those who had walked down the avenue in the opposite direction. All I had was a no man's land that was too small for me to consider taking action just then. My terrified exaltation had vanished with the efforts of chasing the man and I was now sustained only by an icy determination. Only external circumstances could cause me to fail.

It took us a long time to pass all those people I would have cheerfully trampled. When the leaders were far behind us, I realized that the prey had trapped the hunter. He twisted his head and shoulders around quickly and something in his jerky gait made me think he was starting to panic.

I pulled my tie out of my coat pocket and wrapped an end around each hand. But, given the man's seeming awareness of his imminent danger, I no longer felt I could complete the deed. The man could turn around and cry out for help or he could start to run and I would become the prey.

My assurance and my clarity of thought, which I had regained with so much difficulty, were starting to abandon me. I threw my tie away and quickened my pace. It seemed to me as if my arteries had doubled in diameter, that an enormous torrent boiled through them and I was about to rush the old man furiously.

In a flash, I adapted to the new situation. I saw myself rolling about with him in the snow, shattering his skull against the edge of the sidewalk and disappearing immediately, making the most of my lead over those we had passed.

A red mist rose in front of my eyes and my ears were filled with roaring. A taxi drove by slowly. The man crossed the avenue in two strides, opened the taxi door and jumped in. The taxi drove off immediately. I came to a stop, one foot in a gutter filled with broken ice, as the man who would accuse me the next day vanished in his miraculous taxi.

I set off slowly, shoulders hunched, dragging my heels. My murderous madness was lifted from me, as a coat is removed, and I do believe I felt no despair over my failure. In fact, I felt considerably relieved. The terrible sense of guilt that had washed over me few seconds earlier had fled along the same road as my victim and, while I felt a terrified resignation when thinking about the future, I was relieved that I had escaped from myself. Despite my fears being stronger than ever, I thanked destiny for preventing me from becoming a criminal.

Now I had to go back to my home and the person I shared it with, I would have to account for my gloomy mood, submit to countless questions and protests of disbelief, all at a time when I needed solitude and time to regain my sanity.

Good grief! Flanders had also seen Heiligenshtadt. He had seen *Tragic Philosophies* as well and he knew the names of the characters. We'd both seen the incredible change that had occurred in the text, after the German had unbelievably materialized straight out of Clara

Conway's mind. During the course of her existence, had the author of the book actually had one foot in the spirit world and was the work she had penned part of some formidable secret that allowed it to play a role in human lives today? But that was only the first part of the problem! The presence of my cadaver in Flanders' office posed another problem that was just as difficult. Filled with anguish, I wondered how the situation could be resolved. Perhaps my need to understand the true meaning of *Tragic Philosophies* surpassed my fear of what lay ahead of me...

Nearby, a coffee house offered a brightly lit refuge. I went in, walking like a robot, moving without transition from a terribly, icy world, into one filled with warmth, smoke, clinking glasses and conversations. I leaned against the counter and ordered a cognac. The following moments erased part of my anxiety.

CHAPTER III

I first set foot on French soil during the liberation and I had never left it. Before the war, I worked as an editor at the BBC, in a department that provided cultural programs intended for France and, as a result of some odd sort of symmetry, the day following the armistice, I obtained a similar position, in Paris, with the French broadcasting corporation, only this time the programs were intended for my fellow countrymen. Since nothing tied me to London, I had pursued this similar career and left fog and beer behind without any regrets.

Flanders' situation was relatively different, but I could not say exactly how since I had only known him for a year and he was nothing more to me than a contact to help with research. I do believe that our common nationality had originally drawn us together and that a certain manner of looking at events, from the outside, had contributed to the development of a sort of friendship between us. Steve Flanders had not been in France as long as I had. He was 37 years old and a widower. He was short, his face continued to look young, he was most amiable and he was not made for the solitary life that I found quite satisfactory, at least until Jenny came into my life.

Jenny Serenzac, the least English of the three of us, had a French father. Her mother had landed in a village in the province of Béarn during the time of the Irish revolution, after fleeing from Dublin where her life was in danger. When she arrived in Paris, at the age of 20, Jenny almost immediately crossed my path and I took her under my wing. Since she had good taste, I introduced her to the artistic director at a department store who, over the past year, had employed her as one of his many window dressers. The salary she received was not generous, but she was learning a trade she enjoyed and she would eventually be able to live independently.

I left the smokey bar as it was about to close and once again found myself on the snow-covered sidewalk, in a deserted, silent city where I felt I had only enemies and no friends.

For a brief moment, I considered hailing a taxi, but soon abandoned that idea. The later I got home the better it would be. What I found the hardest was that, in the year I had been living with Jenny, I had gradually abandoned my fierce determination to remain single and, for some time now, I had been considering marriage and who knows that else. What's more, I had got so carried away by this new decision that I felt all the more overwhelmed by the extraordinary event that would be covered by all the newspapers the next day. No matter how things went, it would be a catastrophe.

Was it too late to try something? I had already furiously followed a man with the plan to kill him. What was to keep me from returning to the library, where I knew the door was unlocked, in an effort to make the compromising cadaver disappear?

I slowed down, then stopped with my back to the street. In a store window, I saw my image, violently lit by a streetlamp. I stood under the light, motionless. I jumped, startled. In the window I clearly saw my reflection, that of a man bundled up against the cold, but my head and my hat had been replaced by an abominable caricature with twisted features, bulging eyes and two long, canine teeth hanging over my lower lip. I moved closer to the window, both fascinated and incredulous. The store sold costumes. By some curious optical allusion, the reflection of my head seemed to coincide with a very real hideous mask displayed in the window at human height. There was something strange about the fact that it was the only mask on display. Given my troubled state of mind, I took it as a warning, as if the coming days held some frightful metamorphosis for me.

I set off, once again heading for the library. I walked quickly toward the banal place that had served as a theater for such exceptional events and, as so frequently happens under such circumstances, I thought that time slowed or sped up in keeping with the events occurring. A four-hour trip by train, drowsing in a compartment, growing impatient, seems like just a few minutes when you read a book from cover to cover. Likewise, the chase that had brought me to this place, through some strangely inverted process, had seemed to last an eternity and I believed I was kilometers away from my starting part. In actual fact, the avenue was not a long one and I found myself at my destination without having time to consider what I was about to do.

I pushed the large door once again and it opened silently. I did not turn the light in the staircase on. I was sufficiently familiar with the place that I was not afraid that I would trip or would have to fumble my way about. I did not turn the lights on in the reading room either and I approached Flanders' office in the dark. There, standing in front of the door lit by the ghostly light of the snow that came in through the window, I was overwhelmed by an anxiety even more intense than during my initial visit. I had to force myself to move ahead. I walked cautiously over to the window, taking care to follow the walls and the stacks of books and, above all, making sure I did not walk straight across the distance that stood between me and the office, where I knew a body was lying.

I glanced carefully through the window, making sure no one was down below who could see the light. After that, I walked back to the door and pressed on the light switch.

My body was still there, inert, frozen in the same position. I turned the lights off immediately.

I still had not considered exactly how I would do it, but I knew there was only one solution. I had to make it disappear. Suddenly, all of the fears that had overwhelmed me in the previous hours seemed groundless. If someone discovered the body, no one would think to invent some story about a double. They would simply consider me dead, as long as no one discovered me at home during the course of the investigation. The only thing I definitely feared was the loss of my identity. But I immediately realized that my existence would be complicated considerably by the fact that I could not continue to live when everyone believed I was dead. This meant losing my job, all my social contacts, with the exception of Jenny, although she would wonder what had happened to me. All this made it much easier for me to try to make my double disappear than if I had acted under the influence of the terror that had overwhelmed me earlier. I clearly saw that, with a little bit of effort and some skill, I could completely eliminate any trace of my strange adventure. And doing so would not prevent me from continuing my efforts to discover the ins and outs of the matter.

The idea that came to me would enable me, if I managed to bring it to fruition, to erase any trace of the enigmatic cadaver: in the basement of this over-heated building, there must be a central furnace I could use as a crematorium.

With a great deal of difficulty, I placed my look-alike's body on my shoulders and felt the icy head wobble against my neck. I stumbled through the reading room and started to walk heavily down the stairs. As I approached the ground floor, I grew more and more frightened at the thought of seeing something that looked so much like me twist and burn in the flames, in a terribly realistic vision of hell.

When I reached the ground floor, I let the body slip to the floor. A few meters away, the glass door that looked onto the sidewalk provided enough light to allow me to search for a door leading to the basement. On a purely intellectual level, I remained lucid and in control but, when it came to the uncontrollable area of sensitivity, a thousand contradictory emotions surged through me, setting my nerves on edge and covering my face with sweat. Feeling my way along the wall, I discovered a rather low door which, unlike the others, resisted when I tried to open it. After several fruitless attempts, I realized the key was still in the lock. As I pulled the door toward me, the power turned on somewhere at the bottom of the stone staircase that wound down in a spiral, as revealed by the last rays of the dim light that rose in my direction.

I took two steps back, heart pounding with fear, imagining that someone, who had been hiding in the dark cellar, had rushed over to the light switch as soon as he heard the door open. But since everything remained silent, I supposed, as much a result of logical thinking as a need for comfort, that an automatic device lit up the basement as soon as someone started down the stairs. I decided to reconnoiter before once again picking up my sinister burden, so as to avoid wasting my energy in the event that the heating system was too modern to be of any use to me.

I stepped down onto the first step and carefully closed the door, fearing that someone would walk into the lobby at any moment and discover the body I had left there. I started walking down the stairs cautiously, barely able to control the trembling of my hands. I was not all that convinced that the light had turned on all on its own and I was prepared to fight to the finish if someone leapt out at me. When I lost sight of the door through which I had entered, I picked up my pace, thinking that the light might go out. But nothing of the sort happened and I reached the foot of the staircase without any problems.

I found myself in a corridor measuring a few meters long and containing three large doors, one on each side and the other at the end. Since the two side doors most likely opened onto cellars that were of no interest to me, I walked toward the one at the end of the corridor. This door was protected by a large lock. I feared I would be unable to open it then realized that the hinge screwed to the wall was very loose. I set to work on it and, after ten minutes, scraping my fingers and breaking my fingernails, I managed to undo it. The door finally opened, revealing a vast cellar, which was also lit. Inside, an average sized furnace purred gently. Seeing the enormous pile of charcoal, or rather coke, which reached up to a closed cellar window, I realized the heating system did not use oil. I made sure that I could open the furnace door easily. That done, I walked up the stone staircase quickly and returned to the lobby which was still dark.

Draped over my shoulders, the cadaver seemed even heavier than it had earlier. My legs collapsed under me and I almost broke my neck on the stairs.

When I stepped into the furnace room, I released the body so abruptly that it fell violently, the head striking the cement floor with a dull thud, that echoed through my skull. Terror filled me at the disgusting thought that anything that was done to the body could have repercussions on my own.

After pulling an iron rod to open the furnace door, I had to protect my head and hands from the terrible heat pouring out of it. Once again, I despaired. The furnace was ten times too small for the body. I looked at the thing in horror. I would have to butcher it in a rather bloody manner and place the debris among the burning coals.

Bile rising in my throat, I stepped back. Butchering what was sort of my twin brother was beyond me. I had depleted all my energy for nothing. Whether the body was found in the cellar or in Flanders' office changed nothing at all. And there was no way I could complete my horrible task. Overwhelmed by a limitless sense of discouragement, I let myself slip down to the floor and remained there, looking back and forth from the furnace and the thing I had dragged into the cellar. In fact, it was not just disgust that kept me from acting, but also fear, a feverish fear of what I would experience when chopping up and something that looked just like me and then throwing it into the furnace. I thought of French serial killer Henri Landru and finally wondered if I might just have lost my mind.

Still, I had to find some way out of this impasse. I finally opted for a solution that was almost just as repugnant, but which did allow me to reach my goal. All I had to do was burn the hands of the cadaver so that it would be impossible recognize the fingerprints and, if necessary, push the head into the furnace and let the flames disfigure it. In that way, all anyone would find would be an anonymous cadaver whose fate would be of no interest to me.

I stood up awkwardly, bristling at the thought of what I was about to do. I grasped the body under the armpits and dragged it in the blinding light to the furnace. Its door was open, revealing a magma of red coals and short flames. I thought that the furnace had been loaded to burn through a good part of the night although normally there was no reason to heat the library until it opened. No doubt, the municipality wanted the building to be warm when the first readers arrived in the morning.

I used both hands to lift the cadaver's left arm and move it towards the flames. But I cried out in fear and pain, dropping the body which fell face down on the floor. A sharp burning sensation crossed through my fingers.

I stood there, horrified and dumbfounded. The waves of fear I had imagined all came true in a flash. It was impossible for me to touch the terrible thing without feeling the results myself. I remained there, stunned, for several minutes. No matter what happened, I could never touch that thing again and if someone decided to torture those diabolical remains, I would suffer the consequences, much like if someone had made a clay effigy of me in order to cast a spell over me. I don't believe stories about bewitching and effigies which people hammer nails into. But, in the case at hand, I had to accept the obvious. Whether I wanted to or not, those things that came out of nowhere apparently gave anyone power over me which I had no weapon to fight. I decided to leave everything as it was because the best thing that could happen to me was for someone to bury my effigy as quickly as possible. Even under those conditions, a frightful idea sprang into my mind: once my double was placed in his grave, what would happen to him? No doubt what happens to all cadavers: it would be attacked by worms. Would I, while still alive and without my health being affected, suffer the millions of pains caused by the creatures roaming through the body of the unresponsive cadaver?

I started pacing feverishly back and forth, in a state of indescribable panic. When I managed to think more clearly, I realized that I had stupidly latched on to the secondary question concerning the cadaver while the core of the problem lay in *Tragic Philosophies*.

It seemed to me that I was cornered in a burrow that was about to be smoked out... It was not the smoke I should be angry about, but those making it. I would never rest before I had met Heiligenshtadt once again.

I left the library, frightened, feeling more desperate than I had ever felt before. My situation was filled with such an infernally dark horror far surpassing that of even the most pitiless verdict. Even worse, there was nothing to give me hope that I would talk with Heiligenshtadt again and that I was not actually caught in the hands of a cadaver that looked just like me.

The cool night air gradually brought me back to my senses... Why had I not thought about the book earlier? I raced back into the building, pressed the switch, flooding the staircase with light, with no thought about rousing the curiosity of passersby, and raced up the stairs three at a time.

In the reading room, I rushed over to the table I had worked at earlier. The book was no longer there. Flanders had put it away before leaving, in the closed stacks. I rushed over to the door of the large room he had taken me into. This door was the only one in the building that had been carefully locked.

I walked back down the stairs, as if sleepwalking, leaving all the lights on behind me. If I had found the book, I would have rushed to burn it in the furnace and, all things considered, I would have perhaps committed a fatal error. By asking Flanders for a book that Leadbeater mentioned somewhere, I had placed my finger in a gear and I was now caught in it up to my wrist.

I walked on the snow with a choppy step and through the icy wind that tore at my face, I thought I heard, somewhere in the ground or in the sky, the dull purr and metallic clicking of some immense shredder as I felt my body being slowly drawn into it.

After racing wildly for 30 minutes, I finally arrived at my home.

While I was searching for my keys, I was surprised to hear the sound of voices on the other side of the door. It was late at night and Jenny was not alone! I refused to eavesdrop at the door like a servant and noisily inserted my key in the lock. The door opened. As I stepped into the dimly lit vestibule, first Flanders, then Jenny, approached, both waving their arms.

Steve was talking loudly but I didn't initially understand what he was saying, as I focused on Jenny whose fine blond hair stood out against the black silk dressing gown she wore and the burgundy color of the wall behind her. I didn't understand why she was so very pale. She didn't say a word, looking at me with large dark eyes filled with joy mingled with fear.

I walked over to her, started to embrace her and only then did I turn to Flanders and pay attention to what he was saying.

"It's… It's you, Crawson," he said, eyes filled with terror. "I thought you were dead!"

I turned my head slightly and looked at him side-wise.

"What do you mean?" I asked.

"But… but," he finally said. "Where have you come from? You left me in the reading room and you left the building before me. I presume you recall that?"

"No doubt," I murmured, looking at Jenny.

He glanced quickly at the young girl then returned his eyes to me.

He continued, saying "A few minutes after you left, while I was putting that famous book back in the closed stacks, I heard footsteps in the reading room. I walked out of the closed stacks and into the large reading room, but there was no one there. Intrigued, I wondered if the extravagant character you had talked to me about and shown me, sitting at the edge of the fountain, could be there. It was only when I went into my office that I saw you lying on your back on the floor, apparently dead. Fear gripped me and I lost all control of myself. I hesitated for a moment as I considered calling the police, but the fear of getting involved in murder prevented me from doing that. I came to your place, both to gain time and inform Miss Serenzac about the terrible event I thought I had witnessed.

"Fletcher!" said Jenny in a quiet voice.

I pulled her close and she burst into tears against my chest. I lifted my head up and glanced at Steve who was watching us stealthily.

"Well, well…" he said, hesitantly. "So, you came back upstairs? You felt unwell in my office and I thought you were dead when you had only fainted?"

"No!" I replied. "Nothing like that happened. I apologize, but I can't give you a lengthy explanation this evening. I suggest you read the newspapers that will come out tomorrow morning, or rather this morning, in a few hours."

He stepped back.

"Fine!" he said. "Fine! I'll leave you be!"

He was obviously looking for something to say, unable to find anything appropriate.

"I'll leave you be then," he finally said. "Good night. I hope you're feeling better."

He took a few steps back, saluted, and walked off.

I stared at the door he had just walked through feeling as every single word he had just uttered was pure invention. Obviously, he had lied with impunity, disguising everything, transforming everything, but why?

I turned back to Jenny, and pulled her to the back of the apartment, while caressing her hair.

CHAPTER IV

The next morning, the newspapers mentioned my adventure of the previous night, but not at all as I had feared. I found nothing more than a snippet stating that strangers had got into a municipal library somehow, leaving the lights on and the furnace door open, making no mention of the body I had abandoned in the basement. Either the police had decided to make no mention of the matter to the journalists or my double had somehow disappeared! I had spent the whole night panicking for nothing. It had taken me over an hour to calm Jenny and Flanders must have searched through the columns of print, dumbfounded, looking for something that would explain my attitude the previous evening.

How stupid I was! Steve was not looking for anything of the kind. He was aware of everything. He knew more than I did. Had I not seen him talking with Heiligenshtadt through the reading room windows? Had I not recognized my own silhouette standing with them? Hadn't his words been obvious?

I left a calm, comforted Jenny at 10 o'clock and ran to the library just as it was about to open.

The weather was turning bad. The temperature had risen a few degrees, transforming the beautiful white snow of the previous evening into a disgusting, icy slush. I arrived at the library, feet wet and cold, in a bad mood.

I had two important reasons for going back there. First, I felt a need to go back down into the basement, a need that was completely ridiculous since the police had already come and gone, obviously erasing all signs of what they had kept hidden from the journalists. But that made no difference. At the same time, there was something much more important, my possible counter-attack. And I could only undertake that counterattack by asking Flanders to give me *Tragic Philosophies* again. Of course, I didn't presume that having the book in my hands would free me once and for all. But it would be a starting point and I might find something interesting in it.

Steve greeted me oddly and I found something restrained in his attitude. Pretending a deep interest in the contents of the newspapers, I asked him for a copy of the form authorizing me to go down into the basement, which he gave me, protesting that I had no need to inform him and if that was what I wanted it was the least he could do for me.

I went down to the basement immediately but, as I had expected, I found absolutely nothing of interest. The cadaver had vanished just as mysteriously as it had appeared. But Flanders had to know more than I did about the matter... Yet, I said nothing to him about what I was thinking and moved onto my second concern. At my request, he located the large, shabby book and handed it to me. I leaned against his desk and we glanced through a few pages together.

Something in the text struck us like an arrow. From his expression, I clearly saw that he had been affected as strongly as I was. Was he faking again?

Heiligenshtadt's character was once again part of the plot.

I stood up and stared at the wall in front of me, without seeing it. Next to my elbow, I felt Flanders head. He had remained seated and was watching me stealthily.

As I glanced at him, he quickly turned his eyes back to the book and started to murmur something indistinct.

"That Clara Conway," I suddenly said. "Do you have any idea at all what she really does? What kind of person was she in her day?"

He stood up and walked over to a pile of books.

"She must have been a very mysterious woman," he said without turning back. "In the little that has been written about her, she comes across as some sort of magician who never ran afoul of anyone other than the church, as a result of her powerful supporters at the Court... In any case those that met her in person described her as very beautiful and intelligent. But, above all, they said she was dangerous and communicated with spirits."

"Beautiful?" I asked. "At what period in her life? Did she die young?"

"No one knows when she died. Some claimed that went to live with demons without really dying. In any case, there is no trace of her after she reached her thirties. Leadbeater, as you may have noticed yourself, has serious reservations about her."

"No doubt, no doubt...' I said, in an approving tone.

But what was more important at that time was Flanders' awkward and uncomfortable attitude rather than the details he was providing about the author of *Tragic Philosophies*.

I walked over to him and abruptly said, "So, you didn't see Heiligenshtadt last evening?"

He turned about as if I had jabbed a needle between his ribs.

"What do you mean?" he asked, in a voice he intended to be dry and aggressive.

"Nothing. Your attitude last night was a little suspicious. And there's something odd about your behavior this morning. I sense some sort of hypocrisy or malevolence."

He remained silent. Obviously, he seemed to be finding it hard to choose between making some sort of indignant counter-attack or a whiny protest.

"You think so?" he finally said. "And what exactly are you criticizing me for?"

"I think you're lying. It's as simple as that. I'm convinced that you saw our fabulous character yesterday, after I left, since I saw you both from where I was standing, as I was examining the footsteps in the snow. You were standing by the windows, deep in conversation and your silhouettes were quite easy to recognize. Why would you take such pains to hide that from me? What were you plotting with Heiligenshtadt?"

He remained silent for a moment, pretending to look through the pages in Leadbeater's book.

"I hadn't intended to let you know..." he finally said, in a dull voice. "I didn't want to upset you."

I burst out laughing. A nervous, insulting laugh, surprising myself.

"Really?" I hissed. "And now that you've acknowledged that conversation to me, would you please tell me what you were discussing? I imagine that friends as new as you and Ulrich can't have too many secrets."

He glanced me, eyes filled with hatred.

"What do you know about indiscretion, he said, bitterly.

I clenched my fists and grumbled, "And would it also be indiscreet to ask you about myself? And would it be considered vicious for me to try and find out why you spoke to me about the cadaver as if you had found it lying cold in your office when I *saw* my double standing at the reading room window between you and Heiligenshtadt? I'm sorry, but I must conclude that you took part in the death of that double which only you and I have seen and which has now disappeared. You don't think the matter concerns me just a little?"

He glanced at his watch and looked and looked back up with an air of bravado.

"You're too curious," he said, brutally. "But I am not going to give you any satisfaction. The dice have been cast and no matter what you learn, nothing will change the course of events."

I glared at him, thinking he was being evasive yet again.

But he continued, in a louder voice, saying "The events you have witnessed since yesterday are only the culmination of a series of maneuvers that I have been carefully setting up over the past year. When I saw Jenny Serenzac for the first time, I wondered why such a beautiful girl had fallen into your hands while I was still alone following the death of my wife. It was obvious that she had encountered you simply by chance and that she could just as easily have belonged to me. I was just as capable as you of preparing her for life and I would have felt no need to use such a hypocritical excuse to hide a relationship which I would have promptly made legitimate."

I closed my eyes halfway and, barely containing my rage, I said, "All this just to tell me how disappointed you are?"

He ignored the interruption.

"Now, barely six months ago, I discovered an apocryphal pamphlet that provides the key to *Tragic Philoso-*

phies, which I had read a long time ago. The key gave me the most elegant of weapons to use against you."

"Namely?" I asked, voice dripping with irony.

He paused for a second and smiled smugly.

"Let's suppose..." he said. "Let's suppose that the characters in this book are in some way souls in hell... Clara Conway had no shortage of enemies. But she vanquished them in a terrible manner. She wrote a book and named her characters after the people she wanted to destroy. Not only did they disappear as she mentioned them in her book, but they also found themselves bound there, in the sense that in a place men cannot reach, the framework and the plot of *Tragic Philosophies* really do *exist.*"

I shrugged.

"You poor idiot!" I shouted. "Are you hoping that Heiligenshtadt's appearance is enough to make me swallow such a ridiculous tale?"

He raised his eyebrows.

"I don't hope anything at all,' he said calmly. "The very near future will open your eyes. But note that the main character, the one you have just named, the one who behaves in such an odious, sadistic manner in the book was one of Clara Conway's most powerful enemies. I'm not even certain that the name he bears is not some sort of pseudonym hiding the true identity of the man who made all of the courts in Europe tremble: Cagliostro. In any case, he is the only one our dear Clara manage to bewitch completely. Now, this is where you come in. Ulrich had an escape route in the event that the book fell into the hands of a reader whose astrological firmament was identical to his own. In that case, he could escape from the book by being replaced. You are that unfortunate reader and you will, willingly or forcibly, replace Heiligenshtadt."

A sort of superstitious fear washed over me. The archivist's nonsense was starting to sound all too plausible for my taste.

I managed to adopt an ironic tone again.

"Don't you think that your method for getting rid of a rival is just a bit too complicated to come from a healthy mind?" I asked in a calm voice, that hid an overwhelming desire to flee.

"I don't," he said simply. "I don't for the very good reason that I'm not inventing anything and I am simply making good use of a secret I discovered by chance. I focused on giving you advice about some of Leadbeater's books which mention *Tragic Philosophies*. I showed no eagerness to see you read them so as not to rouse your suspicions... Quite naturally, you asked me for Clara Conway's book, which I gave you without the pamphlet... You may recall that I first asked you for your birth date... As you can see everything was quite clear and I had no need to develop what you refer to as complicated methods."

I controlled myself with difficulty and walked over to him.

"I pity you more than I hate you," I shouted in his face. "With respect to your story, either you have a sick imagination or you are exorbitantly credulous. I forgive you for your interest in Jenny because you will never have her, particularly behaving as you do!"

I took two steps back and was preparing to leave when I stopped, reconsidering.

"Since you are divulging confidences, please explain what my cadaver was doing here last night," I asked.

He frowned.

"Oh! I can explain that," he said. "Although it does mean a partial failure on my part. In any case, next time... This is it. In order to be replaced, Heiligenshtadt, needed a double of you. He made another Fletcher Crawson materialize before my eyes... but that operation exhausted him. He was not able to give it a sustainable existence and the double collapsed after a few minutes, after first moving about in an incoherent manner, much like a poorly operated marionette. The cadaver remained there all night, then returned to the void. Heiligenshtadt no doubt made contact with the current reality for a few hours then had to return to his book. He explained to me that this double was an integral part of the process he had to use since he needed a transition between you and the Crawson you would become, 'down below'. It's a sort of two-part transfer. First, you incarnate your double, who is already a part of the supernatural essence. Then you move into your new framework, which will be the final one. Heiligenshtadt hid nothing from me because he will finally be able to free himself through me."

I didn't say a word, just turned about and strode out of the office. As I hurried between two tables, I almost knocked over a tiny, stunted old lady, bending her head, with its bun and glasses, over a double-paged illustration of the sinking of the Lusitania.

I was in such a state that, instead of making even the slightest apology, I looked at her, furious, and chortled as I barked, "So, I thought you were never going to set foot in this library again?"

She blinked, smiled maliciously and uttered words that took my breath away.

"You young idiot," she said. "Instead of harassing an old woman, you should pay attention to your reading."

I tried to make her explain what she meant, but she went back to her contemplation of the rescue boats sinking with their cargos around the transatlantic liner in distress. I was unable to make her say another word.

As I left the library, I involuntarily thought about what Flanders had told me about Clara Conway.

"No one knows when she died..."

Along my way, I considered the archivist's extraordinary tale. In a somewhat threatening manner, it did account for what had been happening since the previous night. However, in light of Flanders' new attitude, it could be considered a blustery web woven to determine just how attached I was to Jenny.

The German—whose clothing, although somewhat outdated, looked nothing like the outfits worn in the 18th century—might be nothing more than a pawn manipulated by Flanders to provide a backdrop for his storytelling. From that point of view, my own cadaver gave me a harder time. I was unable to figure out how the two accomplices had come up with such a cadaver, particularly one that was identical to me... The terrifying repercussion I had felt in my own body when I had tried to burn the cadaver could, in a pinch, be explained by autosuggestion, but that meant bypassing the real problem. Heiligenshtadt's disappearance from Flanders's office the previous evening remained an enigma... And now the strange words uttered by the old woman, which seemed to prove that she was aware of my adventure...

No, all in all... No matter how hard I tried to view the matter in terms of concrete reality and simple human passions, I still stumbled over two or three events for which there was absolutely no explanation.

The snow had almost melted away. From the bus where I found myself, people with closed faces, focused on their own problems, watched absently as buildings flowed past. On both sides of the vehicle, the tires threw slush at the passersby as they tried to avoid it, swearing or shouting in indignation. When I got off the bus, I felt as anonymous as all those beings I had glimpsed for a moment and just as alone with my own concerns. In fact, I probably felt more alone than they did.

I walked up the stairs slowly, preparing to treat Jenny as I had treated Flanders. Of course, his presence in my home, the previous night, could be explained, particularly from Steve's point of view. But I thought I saw something more like fear than joy in Jenny's expression when I had walked into my place. I promised myself I would question her in turn, to determine the exact nature of her relationship with the archivist. During the part of the night I had spent with her, I had not thought of doing so since my suspicions concerning Flanders were still so vague.

I reached my front door, put the key in the lock and opened the door. Usually, the vestibule was rather poorly lit, but it seemed even darker then. I stepped in and closed the door. As my eyes adapted to the darkness, I imagined that Jenny had had to close the shutters in the dining room and the bedroom for some reason or other and I took a few steps ahead.

I stopped short. I was not in my apartment. The vestibule was much narrower than mine was and I could not see the openings that normally provided access to the two rooms through which the light came in. Yet my door had opened the strange door. I retreated, somewhat worried about being caught in a neighbor's apartment. The door opened slowly when I pushed it. I stepped back from it in fear. The door did not look out onto the landing but into an immense parlor plunged in semi-darkness.

The sensation of depersonalization, of an abominable nightmare, that embraced me froze my feet to the floor.

"I was... I was in the staircase just a minute ago," I stammered out loud. "And now this door, this door that I have opened, provides no access to either the staircase or my apartment!"

I turned back. Behind me stood the same, strange corridor. I took two steps in the other direction. I was still facing the same parlor, one I had never seen before...

One I had never seen ever, no doubt! However, it seemed to recognize me. Dumbfounded, I remained frozen, looking for a way out of this inexplicable situation. I was not even in an impasse. Since an impasse has at least one end. Here, the two paths, one in front of me and the other behind me, had disappeared simultaneously.

Soon another impression forced its way into my mind. My clothing. The shape and the texture were unknown to me... Unknown. Well, perhaps not actually unknown!

I realized it immediately. The clothing, ageless and shapeless, was that worn by Heiligenshtadt! I had never seen the parlor before, but I had *read* about it. Flanders had not been bluffing. I was caught in a trap.

Over the next few minutes, I felt an unbelievable sensation of fatality sweep over me. While conserving my entire inner being, I was going to have to obey superior injunctions while some imperious force was already trying to make me take action. I was victorious at the outset, clinging determinedly to the wall, refusing to step away from it under any pretext. But second by second, the successive waves of a foreign personality kept conquering a new section of my nerves and my muscles. I had entered Cagliostro's character in *Tragic Philosophies*. I had become a character in a novel. I had become a puppet whose strings were being pulled by the author. That author was Clara Conway and if, by some trick of magic, she was still alive, she was no longer able to change my destiny which she once and for all cast in her mad pages. What would become of Jenny? What would become of me? Deep down I knew the answers to both questions. Jenny would probably move in with Flanders without too much coaxing. As for myself, I had read quickly through the novel in which I was trapped and since I knew that no human force could change the plot, I was condemned to live up to the last page.

I started walking slowly, first with movements made awkward by the interior anarchy I was struggling against. I walked silently down the frightful corridor that should have been my vestibule. I had no clear vision of what lay ahead of me since I didn't exactly recall the point at which Clara Conway had provided a description of the parlor. At the same time, as I mentioned, I had merely skimmed through *Tragic Philosophies* and was not that knowledgeable about the book. I knew one major thing: taking Heiligenshtadt's place, I was going to commit a host of evil deeds. When I had found within me that murderous drive that had sent me on the trail of an inoffensive passerby, that idea did not displease me. But I was no longer entirely myself and that filled me with such horror that, for a brief moment, I was able to vanquish the internal fatality that my new, mythical personality filled me with. But I had to surrender almost immediately and I continued walking ahead.

At the end of the corridor there was another door. I knocked on it.

"Come in…" called a coarse voice from within.

I opened the door.

In the middle of a vast, richly furnished room lit by several torches a man was pacing back and forth in front of two tall windows through which I saw a landscape of snow-covered forests. The individual was wearing black satin knickers, black stockings, shoes with buckles and a sort of belted vest. White, silky lace hung from his shirt-sleeves and a ruffle of the same lace lay under his chin. He wore a powdered wig tied at the back of his neck with a black velvet ribbon and the sheath of the sword, which tapped against his left leg, shone with a thousand lights. His face, with very coarse features, was extraordinarily white and moved only when he stood still to glare at me, a hand on his hip.

"What's this? Who are you?" he asked. "And how did you manage to get in here without my people coming to warn me?"

"I apologize…" I heard myself say. "My name is Fletcher Crawson, and I share your blood!"

"Fine," he continued in a toneless voice. "Take time to sit down. Then tell me immediately the reason for your visit."

I walked over to a chair with twisted legs, covered with a light gray tapestry portraying a hunting scene. But before I reached it, I was bombarded by a mental explosion filled with limitless despair. Dumbfounded, I turned to look at the margrave. He stood there, motionless and haughty, his face still a pale, inexpressive mask. But in my mind, I heard the silent sentences of his thoughts, choppy phrases filled with pain and rage.

"Imposter, vile imposter... so you're the one, you miserable wretch, that Heiligenshtadt got to take the bait. It's all over for you, and you will never get out of here and here is nowhere, for both the dead and the living. It's a personal hell odiously designed by Conway, may she be three times cursed!"

I uttered words like a robot, requiring no effort of thought, all the while recognizing their architecture, "I am a messenger of the Grand Duke of Bade and, using means I cannot reveal to you, I managed to evade the surveillance of your trackers and the cumbersome diligence of your lackies..."

But just as I was pronouncing those pompous syllables, my thoughts meandered in a very different direction. Flanders had been right about everything. Like the other prisoners in this world of nightmares, I was subjected to the plot, the facts and the dialogue of *Tragic Philosophies*. And just like them, I had kept my personality and it was telepathy that, like a watermark and between the lines, provided the real language for these apparent men.

"... until the end of this enormous book."

Frightfully painful laughter rang out in my mind.

"Poor fool," said the margrave, continuing with his mechanical conversation. "You have not been here long enough to know that the duration of the tale has frozen into ice around us, like running water freezes in the winter wind. You are not here with us until the end of this bewitched book, but until the end of time! Soon enough, you'll see that in our world there is no future, just an eternal present, that the conscious vision of each of us simultaneously embraces the first lines of this demon book and the very last words."

Terror filled me. When I had attempted to burn the fingers of my double's cadaver, when I felt the pain, I had thought no other situation could be more horrible than that. I was wrong. A fate a thousand times more atrocious awaited me. Without dying I had been condemned to hell and the person I had replaced was joyfully moving into the life I had left behind forever. I coldly continued my explanation for my visit, but at the same time, I tried to return to the telepathic conversation we had had, since the possibility of us communicating seemed to me to be the only way to escape from a part of the demented world in which I was trapped.

"Enough!" ordered the margrave in my mind. "We will no longer be able to communicate. We only managed to do so before because you were still not one of us. You will become like us, locked within yourself, condemned to constantly repeat the same nonsense, perform the same sacrilegious gestures of the libertine whose place you have taken. Goodbye! The pit has been dug. Live your death without wakening since dementia is forbidden here."

With that, my existence, if it can be called that, started. In order to escape from the obsessions of the supreme condemnation, I tried to take an interest in my actions and take part in them. I knew full well why I had come to the castle of the margrave, Walter von Horst. Yet, contrary to what the margrave had told me, I had lost track not only of the reasons for my behavior but also any memory of *Tragic Philosophies*. The very title of the book barely flittered about in my memory. And instead of possessing the tortuous omniscience I had been threatened with, every action I performed was unexpected and the characters I encountered all came at me out of the blue. I don't know if this privileged situation was the result of the fact that I came into the situation as an intruder and I had only partially integrated the body of this gigantic evil, but it did allow me to bear the infernal condition I had been thrown into by destiny with less suffering.

When I left the office, the spoken conversation I had taken part in came back to my mind. I had informed the margrave of Hesse that people working for the Grand Duke of Bade were on their way to his castle to kidnap his daughter Frida, that I was the Grand Duke's messenger and my mission was to quell his suspicions and that I was betraying the Grand Duke as a result the heinous crime he planned to commit. I also informed the margrave that the soldiers were still a day's ride away and that he had time to protect his daughter. He replied that, if what I said was true, he would reward me with a high position in his domain and that I would not have to fear the vengeance of my former master.

I went out a different door than the one I had gone in through and found myself in a corridor that was much wider than the first. It was well lit by torches and the walls were almost completely covered by Venetian mirrors.

I caught sight of myself in one of them and my appearance barely surprised me. I had the same pale, frozen face as von Horst. I moved with a strange sliding gait and, as I walked past parallel mirrors, I saw my image multiplied to infinity on each side of myself, walking through endless corridors.

When I reached the massive door at the end of the corridor, I glanced behind me, then placed my ear against the panel. Although all of my actions were dictated by a supreme authority, I was clearly aware that I was still the same Fletcher Crawson who had taken part in battle, in the real Europe, to wind up in early damnation. This made it all the easier for me to appreciate the enormous silence and the strange nature of objects, like those in dreams. It all contrived to make me feel terribly anxious over the vague thought of what was to come.

In a flash, a shred of memory came back to me. In *Tragic Philosophies*, Heiligenshtadt told Horst, "I share your blood!"

I had used the same sentence when introducing myself and that was absurd. And Horst had called me a vile imposter for that very reason.

How could this fit in with the book in which my name, no doubt, now replaced Heiligenshtadt's every time it appeared! In all likelihood, there must be an explanation elsewhere in the book saying that I was the illegitimate child of an English duke or count and that blue blood knew no borders, putting everything back into balance. I did not have time to fully reflect on that since I opened the large door and slipped into the room lit by a seven-branched candelabra in which long candles burned and sizzled.

On a four-poster bed, from which the burgundy curtains had been torn partway off, a girl wearing a nightgown, lay bound and gagged, struggling weakly. She must have been 23 or 24 years old and the ropes that hugged her white silk garment tightly to her body revealed shapes of incomparable harmony. I initially thought her hair was brown but I quickly realized that the long curls, lying this way and that on her pillow were deep red, almost mahogany. The gag that covered half her face left a slender nose and large dark eyes exposed.

Those eyes stared at me with the same lack of expression I had noticed in Horst's eyes and in my own when I had glimpsed myself in the mirrors.

Five men wearing black cloaks and tattered three-cornered hats stood around the bed, each carrying a large pistol. One of them spoke to me

"You see, Count, your orders have been followed to the letter," he said respectfully. "But I still think that for our security and yours, we should have dealt with her father permanently so that the attendants don't follow us."

"Thank you for your advice, Hans," I said in the same toneless voice. "I intend to inflict a somewhat more bitter punishment on him. Three of you grab the girl. You and the remaining one will come with me. If some valet escaped from us when we came in and tries to hamper us, blow his head off."

Immediately three of my men grabbed Frida Von Horst by the shoulders and ankles, lifting her up while I walked out through a small door located at the back of the room, accompanied by Hans and the remaining mercenary. The others followed us.

We reached a large marble staircase decorated with banners and breastplates and walked down it in silence. From there, we went into the kitchens and left the castle after wrapping our captive in one of my servants' cloaks. Outside the wind was blowing the snow about. My foot bumped something and, looking down at the ground, I saw a cadaver partially trapped in the ice. Other bodies littered the plain forming white lumps on the frozen ground. I knew that all of these people had died of the plague and that the epidemic would only be eliminated through famine, providing manpower for any task, including the burial of the plague victims.

To my right, a black shapeless mass started moving and I saw about 50 knights who, hidden by a fold in the terrain up to that point, had started advancing toward the castle in relative silence.

When they reached the large door, they dismounted and shot the windows out with their pistols. They rushed inside, shouting. I knew what was to follow since I had organized the entire operation. Either I had or perhaps someone else I was replacing had, been an important person in this world no doubt, for whom I served as an obscure captain. Some of the soldiers had been instructed to invade the margrave's apartments, hold him prisoner for half an hour, and inform him that they belonged to the Grand Duke of Bade and his daughter had been kidnapped. They were to make him believe that she would be used as a hostage in the war that Bade was declaring on Hesse, since the Grand Duke's son, who was living in Hesse, was a so-called prisoner of the margrave.

This was a complete fabrication but the result would be clear: the margrave would arrest Bade's heir, triggering a war between the two states. In this way, not only would I keep the girl, who I would torture in all sorts of manners, since that is my nature, but I would also start a war between two countries that were already sorely tested by the plagues and famine, something I was already enjoying in advance.

In the valley where the knights had been hiding, a carriage was waiting for me with three pairs of robust horses. As I was arranging for my prisoner to be installed there, the men who had taken part in the simulated attack, galloped back and we all raced furiously off in the direction of the border with Wurtemberg, where we would be safe.

How could the margrave have isolated himself in this castle without a garrison, without any way to defend an attack?

We were jostled about so roughly in the carriage that I found it very difficult to release Frida Von Horst from her ropes and gag.

"Villain!" she said, without passion. "My father will have you hanged."

Her deep voice, so toneless and expressionless, troubled me so deeply that I had no difficulty turning back into the Crawson of the living world. A sense of pity, mingled with something much stronger, took over my will and victoriously removed the web of blindness that had fallen over my shoulders when I left the margrave. Alas! Although I had managed to separate myself from the thought of this vile, meaningless drama, my actions were still bound by the same fatality since I grabbed the young girl brutally by the hair and twisted until she screamed. That odious act, committed by me against my will, pained me terribly since I only wanted to embrace her and comfort her.

Gradually, my awareness of my true identity melted back into the internal greyness that clouded my mind. I no longer remembered if I would be subject to physical suffering similar to the suffering I caused or even more painful. All I felt was a limitless desolation.

I grabbed a whip that was hanging in the wall of the carriage and struck the young girl on the face three times. I think I experienced the same burning.

"Bitch!" I said. "You will be the cause of a deadly battle. Your father will end his life in a miserable manner and you will be at my mercy in a place where no one will find you."

I continued to insult her and threaten her, but I noticed that her head had slumped onto her shoulder and was lolling from side to side with the jostling of the carriage the six horses were pulling through the night.

With every fiber of my being, I wanted to kiss her. Instead, I slapped her brutally.

The lantern hanging from the roof swung furiously. I poked my head through the window. Around us, the landscape and the forest were so shrouded in darkness despite the ghostly whiteness of the snow. However, I did note that our speed on the rutted road was much greater than would normally be possible for horses. We were racing along like a hurricane and the trees on each side of us sped past so rapidly they looked as if they were hidden in thick fog.

A word leapt into my mind. We were traveling at the speed of a very fast automobile. Automobile? What was that? Where I had I taken that word with the nonsensical etymology from? Moving on its own! A carriage of some sort that could move about as if it were harnessed to hoses pulling it...

It seemed to me that I had once lived a strange existence in a large city lit by extraordinary means. Or was I seeing a glimpse of the future?

I pulled my head back into the carriage. The biting cold of the wind shrieking around us had cut my skin. It was freezing in the carriage but by comparison I found it pleasantly warm.

I left the girl, whose face was turned away from me and invisible, in peace. She moved only when the carriage jerked and bumped. Apart from these abrupt movements of her body, she remained motionless. She did not speak.

She had pulled the cloak I had wrapped her in during the kidnapping tightly around herself and had curled her legs under her for protection against the cold. Her bae feet must have been freezing. She was half sitting half on her knees on the gold-embroidered green cushions, covered from head to toe in the vast black cloak. I felt pity again, along with a painful desire to caress her hair and her shivering shoulders. I repressed that desire knowing that, in my inexplicable madness, I would merely brutalize her again.

The trip dragged on interminably despite our speed. I poked my head outside once again, to urge the driver to spur on the horses... Fear nagged me. Had Horst already sent one of his valets off to the nearest garrison? Was a troop of knights on light horses already tracking us? We still had a way to go before reaching Wurtemberg...

In fact, given the speed we were travelling at, there was little chance that he would catch up with us before we reached the border. At the same time, I knew that the fifty mercenaries armed to the teeth who were galloping behind us would do everything in their power to delay those pursuing us. And the remaining troops had orders to march to Hartzenberg and lay in wait there until the morning. The pass there was so narrow that 50 determined men could hold off a well-trained regiment.

Our infernal speed slowed. All too soon, the horses were reduced to walking. The road was very steep and would continue like that for a long way. Finally, the horses returned to a trot on the uneven terrain and through the window I saw tall rocky walls. A few minutes later, we slowed again as the road ran over a mountain, but that did not worry me. The handful of scoundrels I had ordered to hunker down in Hartzenberg formed a lock behind me.

Finally, after we had picked up our pace and the road conditions improved, I heard the horses whiney, as they were stopped brutally by my driver. At the same time, voices shouted curses and orders. I glanced outside. Knights surrounded us.

One of them, who was carrying a lantern, bent down to open the door. He was wearing a Wurtemberg uniform. I handed him an envelope sealed with black wax.

"Take this to your captain!" I ordered the man. "And be quick about it, I don't have time to waste."

Another knight, whose horse reared up, approached. His decorated uniform was three-quarters covered by a dark cloak, coated with a dusting of snow. He grabbed my envelope from the soldier's hands while the man moved his lantern closer.

Frida Von Horst, who had remained in a sort of faint up to then, suddenly bolted upright and started to shout, "Help! Help! Protect me! This man is a thief! He snuck into my father's castle and kidnapped me. My father is the margrave of Hesse!'

The captain, who had just finished reading my safe-conduct, signed by an illustrious hand, returned it to me without glancing at my captive. He had his men withdraw and our carriage started moving.

We were on Wurtemberg soil.

The horses started to trot. Considering the attitude of the captain and his men, Frida realized that I had friends in powerful places and fell back into her torpor.

The strange thoughts that troubled me from time to time came back into my mind.

"She's in the same situation I am," I thought. "There are certain words she had to say and she said them. She's living another life internally."

I grabbed her by the shoulders and forced her to look at me. For a second, I thought I was going to be able to get into her thoughts and that I would even take her in my arms. Then I backhanded her.

"Whore!" I said. "Daughter of a tyrant! You thought you could count on the help of the border guards! Forget that stupid idea. No one we meet in this territory will ever help you."

She did not say a word, but I saw tears well up on her eye lashes. I knew those tears were real and that a part of her was truly suffering My pain and my shame intensified, but that was just a prelude. The future held a fate for all of us that grew more and more sinister each moment.

We were heading for the winter residence of the Prince of Wurtemberg and I knew we were close to our destination. Yet, when we were stopped a second time and I had to produce my safe-conduct yet again, I did not feel all that close to our goal.

The bouncing of the carriage was less brutal than at the start of our trip, but it was faster and more abrupt. The carriage was rolling over the uneven cobblestones that lined the main streets of Stuttgart. Here and there, lanterns hanging from certain signs and oil street lamps cast puddles of pale-yellow light, that were reflected in Frida's hair as we drove past.

We stopped on a small street in the heart of the city, a street so narrow there was barely enough room for the carriage. My captive and I both got down from the carriage and the driver and his horses raced off to the stables.

The cold was slightly less intense here. However, there were few passersby. I held Frida firmly by the arm, fearing she would do something stupid.

Using a large key, I opened a low door and pushed her through it, into the shadows, ahead of me. She refused to move ahead and I felt her body pressed against mine. I shoved her roughly and she fell forwards, crying out in fright.

Throat taut with anguish, I shouted a name, "Jenny!"

I immediately recognized the intrusion of that unknown existence I had already recalled several times. At the same time, it seemed obvious to me that I had not really shouted. My cry had remained internal. Nothing had transpired in the icy darkness.

I groped about, looking for a tinder box I knew I had placed on a piece of furniture. I found it in a few moments, struck the flint and lit a candle.

The young girl had got up off the floor and was shivering in her large cloak, weeping silently. I looked her up and down and tore the cloak from her. She stood there in her half torn white silk night gown.

Without further ado, I told her calmly, "This evening, a cheerful colleague will take my place. He has permission to do whatever he pleases with you. He and I are the only ones who have the key to this door and you can see for yourself that there are bars on the window."

I sat down on a large bed that took up an entire room in the large room and I was taking out a silver snuff box when a key was inserted in the lock.

The man who stepped in was wearing a white, richly embroidered suit under his cape.

"You made good haste," he said with a slightly French accent. "I didn't expect to find you here already…"

He seemed to either be looking for a name or perhaps refusing to utter it.

"Crawson," he said.

The light of awareness that came to me was fleeting but it was clearer than any of the previous ones.

"Good grief!" I thought. "My name has replaced Heiligenshtadt's name every time it appears in *Tragic Philosophies*. This man, who perpetually starts his ghostly existence over and over, always utters the same name and now, suddenly, for the first time, something stronger than him has put a strange word into his mouth."

I forgot all that immediately.

"De Valpré," I said. "Pleased to see you again."

But Frida cried out in horror. Her dilated eyes stared at the face of the newcomer, whose nose and upper lip were missing.

I turned to her and said, "Mr. de Valpré was unfortunately sliced by a sword at Fontenoy. But that's no matter! Won't the pleasant face the English gave him merely enhance the pleasure of his embrace?"

Paler than ever, she leaned against the wall, moaning in fear and disgust. De Valpré walked over to her and pulled her close. Her frenzied resistance was overcome in a few seconds. When he threw her onto the bed, I believed I saw the grim repeater himself press his hideous face against Frida's.

A long gun with a damasked barrel lay near the candle holder. Would I pick it and shoot the villain? No! I might hit Frida. What about the long dagger hanging on the wall? As I was considering grabbing it, I had to admit that I could do nothing with either the gun or the dagger. Despite my overwhelming desire to seize a weapon, I was unable to move. I saw the steel blade reflect the dancing flames of the candle with murderous intensity. All my muscles tensed to take hold of it but, despite myself, I had to look away from it. Looking around, I caught sight of myself in a Bohemian mirror, cracked along its entire length. I saw the same blank expression on the same pale face. I looked away. De Valpré, had gagged Frida with one hand and torn her clothes off with the other.

Frozen from head to toe, as cold as marble, I tried to close my eyes to escape from the revolting scene that was about to play out when the man stood up and said to me, "I detest easy victories! Go about your business, Crawson. For now, I'll just keep an eye on her."

"Fine," I said. "No doubt you know that there are various tools in the next room. Use them on her as you see fit, but don't go too far so we will be able to start the game over again together."

I could have screamed. My enslaved body had turned into the worst prison I could have ever imagined.

I headed over to the door and opened it. The next moment, I found myself in the street, rushing to a destination that was imposed on me.

I was received in the middle of the night by the prince of Wurtemberg. Our conversation took place in a small office, away from prying ears. The prince confirmed that I should not be concerned about my captive and that he would pay me the 40,000 thalers promised to me as soon as Hesse and Bade were at war. The two small countries were comparable in strength and they would most likely end the struggle completely exhausted. And the prince of Wurtemberg would take advantage of the combatants' weakness to annex both.

As I left the palace, I wondered if my projects would succeed. Would the margrave arrest the Bade crown prince? That would be fine, but not necessary. On another level of awareness, one question kept coming back to mind over and over. What was Flanders' relationship with Jenny? Those strange names had no connection with anything but I could not shake them out of my mind. They were always there. Yet, as I approached Frida's prison, that obsession was replaced by another: had De Valpré tortured her savagely in the tool room?

Several people were standing on the street where's Frida's shack was located. They were waving their arms about and exclaiming indignantly.

The wind tossed a lamp back and forth, and their oversized shadows multiplied their movements in a fantastic manner.

As I approached, I realized what was keeping them there and the reason for the threatening cries. Although smothered somewhat by the thick walls of the building, horrible cries could be heard coming from the house which I was heading towards.

My blood froze. I was afraid to walk farther. It was Frida von Horst's voice. She was in De Valpré's hands. She started by moaning, then screamed at length and her shriek ended in a series of heart-rending sobs. Silence returned, followed by a new wail, that grew louder and louder, transforming into a mad scream.

A troop of uniformed men ran in from the other end of the street. For a moment, I thought they would break in the door, but they did nothing of the sort. They dispersed the crowd, using their rifles to beat them, while I hid in the shadow of a wall.

When the street was deserted again, I set out in turn. Just as I inserted the key into the lock Frida started screaming like an animal being slaughtered. I opened the door swiftly and the screaming stopped abruptly.

I took a few steps and stopped, dumbfounded. It was not the house where I had left Frida with de Valpré.

It was a vestibule with light shining through the French doors. A vestibule I was very familiar with. The one in my apartment. I was amazed, unable to put two thoughts together. I turned back to look at the street. There was no street. Through the half open door, I saw a staircase, my staircase, the one in the house where I lived with Jenny.

HEILIGENSHTADT'S ACCOUNT

I met Clara Conway under circumstances that should have legitimately marked the beginning of a long friendship between us. We were at a small dinner gathering organized by the French regent for his favorites. A dinner during which Clara and I had an opportunity to provide a few samples of our skills and which ended in a most libertine manner in a most comfortable hunting lodge.

Over a few months, I maintained a relationship with Clara, during which time we learned a lot about one another. Only the Court knew anything about our contacts and the most unexpected rumors circulated there. While Clara Conway's name was known outside the borders of France, mine was celebrated throughout all of Europe. And while I had taken the precaution of hiding myself under the title of Count von Heiligenshtadt, many people recognized me as Cagliostro.

During a trip I made to Thuringe, where I had business with the Langrave, I met a wonderful woman with splendid dark red hair. She was the daughter of Margrave Von Horst who reigned over Hesse. Although her father was present and my business was not delayed, I arranged to draw her close enough that she fell into my net. But I had been too confident with respect to my detachment with respect to women and I was caught in my own trap, like a total greenhorn. This first trip provided a framework a for series of gallant adventures during which I had to tear myself from Clara's arms at least 20 times. Yet she eventually heard about the real reason for my travels and she was filled with furious jealousy and mortal spite. The love she felt for me transformed overnight into tenacious hatred. But she held her change in heart from me with diabolical care.

A short while later, she started to write a most unfortunate book. The few pages that fell into my hands did not deceive me. It was a book impregnated with the powers of evil I had been dealing with myself in secret for long enough that I recognized their sulfurous brand where it appeared.

I felt that, despite the renewed tenderness my mistress showed me, I needed to take a few precautions to protect myself against her spells.

Near the small village of Montrouge, I owned a solitary residence buried in greenery. I spent days and days there concentrating on practicing incantations and conducting alchemical research, but I never managed to define the exact danger that was threatening me. Yet I continued to work feverishly to save myself and, at the end of a night filled with shadowy meditation, I knew that I was going to be able to throw the evils that Clara intended for me straight back at her.

Yet, it was too late. The next morning, the framework that had been built around me was replaced by another. I found myself in the empty, inhuman regions that provide access to hell, a person without a will, chained to the sinister imperatives of the drama Clara had designed. All those weeks of struggling had aged me and I remained permanently fixed in my new appearance.

I was surrounded by characters who had crossed my path. But I was filled with boundless despair when I recognized Frida Von Horst among them, chained to same damnation by Clara's fury. With Machiavellian cruelty,

Clara forced me to act like a vicious brute with Frida and the more my love for her grew, the rougher I treated her.

During the night before I was trapped, I had managed to cast a weak spell: I would be freed when a being born on the same day as I was, at the same minute, the same second, although in a different year, would read this hateful book, the manuscript in its initial edition. This was so unlikely that I prepared to suffer in my hell for thousands of years.

One day as I was going to see Horst, who was trapped in the same spell as I was, I suddenly saw myself in a strange world, a world that was real, but existed many, many years after my own time. My efforts had been fruitful, but I still needed to be replaced by some careless fool. I awkwardly regained the use of my power, although I had to try twice before succeeding.

The first being I saw when I returned to the world of humans was precisely the fool who was taking my place. My contact with him was most fleeting and I didn't care if he was a shepherd or a king. Another man, on the contrary was of great interest to me. His name was Flanders and since he declared himself to be the enemy of the first man, I used him cheerfully to implement all the new ideas that were swirling around in my mind.

But when I understood the broad lines of the principles on which the civilization of these small men was based, when I realized the extent to which it was made of unnecessarily complicated pulleys and gears, I saw that I still had a say in the universe from which spiritual forces had been banned and where most people arrogantly ignored everything that could not be reached through mathematics and the five senses.

This curiosity with respect to things that were so different from my own experience kept my thoughts away from a memory of Frida that was far too vibrant for a few days. I followed Flanders who served as a most useful guide for me and was extremely docile. He had no idea that he was a mere puppet in my hands. He could not have served me better if I had hired him as a butler.

One evening, when we were at his place, polishing off a bottle of old wine, I decided to visit the apartment where Crawson had lived before he replaced me. Flanders had considered my offer repugnant but I had such sway over him that he never once thought of refusing. So, we went there together and that is where I met Jenny.

The girl was dressed in an outlandish outfit and wore her hair in a long braid, but somehow I found her attractive for rather obscure reasons that eventually became clear to me. Jenny had lived with Crawson while I was torturing Frida against my will. Now that Crawson was playing the role of torturer, would it not be just for me to replace him in turn! My heart had withered so much that the idea came to me with an intense desire for a new love. I imagined how much I would enjoy inflicting on Jenny what I had been forced to do to Frida. It would be sweet revenge for me. I seized the opportunity when Flanders had stepped out of the room to make a date with her, one she accepted readily. I left the love birds in their nest and returned to Flanders' place where I was staying temporarily.

I met her in a public park the next day at dusk. Although I looked like a man in his forties, she did not protest when I grabbed her familiarly by the waist and showered her with compliments.

"You didn't know Crawson?" she said, after a moment. "He instructed Steve to tell me that he was heading back to England permanently. He did not wish to tell me goodbye in person since he feared he would cave in and, as Steve told me, he had to return to London as soon as possible. I wept for a few days but Steve came over from time to time to comfort me and, since I've met you, I feel calmer than I've ever felt before."

She paused for a moment, then continued, "It's odd, though, there's something strange and unsettling about you. You remind somehow of the crazy person Fletcher said he met in the library…"

"I know nothing about that," I assured her. "Steve said nothing to me."

She waved her hand evasively and turned to look at the trees and gardens surrounding us.

"When I'm with you, I feel like I'm drugged," she added. "I don't even think you have to be here."

Whistles sounded behind us. Jenny stood up from the bench on which we had been sitting. I did the same.

"They're closing the park gates," she said. "We have to leave."

I left her in the street, beseeching her to see me in person once again. I knew she could not refuse.

"We'll have our own little retreat," I promised her. "One that is not the former apartment of the man who abandoned you. I'll be in touch soon."

The next day, I ordered Flanders to buy me a villa in the outskirts of Paris and furnish it. I gave him some gold, which I obtained easily, to finance it all. When everything was ready, I sent Jenny an invitation indicating the address and the date of our next meeting and I settled into the villa. I had no doubt at all that the next day would be memorable.

That evening, as I was waiting for Jenny, the weather was atrocious. A snowstorm pounded the suburb and the wind shrieked around the house like a banshee.

Yet, it was pleasantly warm inside. I disdained all the curious instruments everyone around me used, but I had to admit that the comfort provided was quite unlike what I had known in the past. These people in the future did enjoy their comforts and they knew how to provide them. The light provided by their small glass globes was the most marvelous thing in the world.

I was pacing back and forth when a sharp bell rang out. I went to open the door. The woman who entered in a squall of snow was not the young girl I had been expecting, but an old woman wearing spectacles with her hair tied up in a bun on the top of her head.

"Good evening!" she said with a smile. "How is Frida?"

I took two steps back and felt the blood drain from my face.

"Clara!" I hissed, overwhelmed with fear and amazement

She closed the door carefully and leaned back against the frame.

"I've been in this astonishing world longer than you have," she commented. "Also, as you can see, I know how to put all these inventions to good use and I closed your door to keep the light and heat from spilling out."

I stomped toward her, filled with an overflowing hatred that seemed to fill the entire house all at once.

"Get out!" I roared. "Get out you wild beast!"

She stepped aside.

"Open the door for me!" she said. "I've grown dry and withered and no longer have the strength to move that heavy piece of wood."

I threw myself at the door and tried to pull it toward me. Impossible. It remained closed, as if Clara had installed several locks on it.

Once again, she had caught me off guard. But I had broken the spell and knew that I was risking nothing.

"I suppose you've come here to show me how much you know," I said, flirting a little.

"No!" she replied in the same tone. "I merely wanted to surprise you when you were expecting another. That librarian, Flanders, took umbrage at the attention you paid the Serenzac girl. When I went to ask him a few questions about you, he guessed who I was, without quite understanding how I could still be in this world. I suppose that, for your part, you don't need to guess at how easy it was for me to isolate myself in a place of exile similar to yours, although one that is less dark and much more pleasant!"

"Enough of your sarcasm!" I said, interrupting her. "What do you really want?"

"I'm not looking for a fight," she said. "But I do insist that you leave Flanders and Jenny in peace. They're perfect candidates for some experiments I'd like to perform."

I stared her straight in the eye, glaring with such intensity that she glanced away.

"I'm sorry," I said. "That's precisely why I'm so interested in them. Do whatever you see fit. We'll see which of us is the stronger this time."

There was something terrifying about her hidden anger. I concentrated all my power and will on the door she had so firmly closed. A few seconds later, there was a great smashing sound in the entrance as a squall of icy wind blew in to where we stood.

"You can see that, since you no longer have the strength to open doors, I will gallantly do it for you." I hissed. "The way is clear. You can leave."

It seemed to me that the hatred that burned in her eyes was mingled with a certain fear.

"Farewell," she said. "Just remember that you will never be the stronger one."

And she turned in the direction of the entrance where the large door, torn from its hinges, hung against the wall. She glanced at my workmanship with disdain and walked down the porch steps. She disappeared from sight before she reached the street.

That very night, following Clara's departure, I took measures she would not suspect for a few days to ensure my security, surrounding myself with an occult barrier that would block her extra-sensorial vision. That was essential for the success for the plan I had in mind for taking my revenge on that little jerk Flanders and playing the very game Clara had forced me into with Frida with Jenny instead.

The next day, I went to his place. He welcomed me with the same hypocrisy I had already noted in him and which my enemy had confirmed through her revelations. He was visibly terrified but doing everything in his power to hide that from me.

"I would like to correct any misunderstanding you may have regarding my feelings," I said. "Your little Jenny, who you have been so willing to turn over to my possession, is of no interest to me, apart from a quite legitimate curiosity that I have regarding women of this time…"

He started to protest with the most doubtful eloquence, but I stopped him, saying," To prove to you that I'm not trying to get between you, I would be pleased if you would accept an offer that will definitely bring a smile to your lips, unless you've lost all confidence in me."

His ears perked up, although the expression on his face, which he was trying to conceal, revealed his concern.

"Would you like me to use my powers to deliver her to you?" I asked. "That would be an excellent opportunity for you to free me from the considerable debt I contracted with you the other day when you found a reader for *Tragic Philosophies* that satisfied the conditions for freeing me... I know you did not act out of any sense of altruism. But the debt is still the same.

At the same time, I used all of my power of suggestion to tear down the barriers built in his mind by doubt and distrust. In this way, I guided him, without his realizing it, toward receptiveness to my will.

"I will make the villa I instructed you to buy available to you," I said, hammering in the final nail. "I will invite the two of you there and I will leave you alone, after first making sure that Jenny will not resist you. I want to believe that, once you have finally conquered her, you will no longer need to hide behind those wicked suspicions you feel in my regard... I know, I know... But I forgive you willingly since my attitude toward her could have resulted in fear on your part."

He gave in. I knew that, since he was now under my control, he would no longer be free to find Clara and seek her protection. Protection that, all in all, meant falling from Charybdis' grasp into Scylla's hands.

Then I went to Crawson's apartment where I told Jenny another story. I had to extend the same invitation to her, in case Flanders saw her before coming to my villa. But I assured her that I was inviting the two of them to a small dinner at which, of course, I would be present until the very end. Although she felt no love for Flanders, she did not find him repulsive either. As a result, she was easier to convince than he had been. That was odd enough since, while I wanted to get rid of Flanders as quickly as possible, I also wanted to keep my hands on Jenny. To do that, I would start by preventing her from coming to the very dinner to which I had invited her. I would only show an interest in her during the days and nights following that.

I was focusing more and more on her since I had come up with an idea which I had resolved to dedicate all my energy to. Initially, I had viewed Jenny as an object of pleasure. By combining that perception with my lengthy experience as a torturer, I took great pleasure in the thought of being able to make her an even tastier victim because she was innocent. Then another idea came to mind. Without abandoning my first plan, why wouldn't I try to send her to join Crawson? She could take Frida's place as Crawson had taken mine. That plan posed problems that were much more difficult to solve than my own liberation since Frida's captivity was not conditional. From the outset she had not enjoyed the possibility of remission as I had... However, I did not give up hope. A certain sort of balance seemed to be developing between Clara and myself that would authorize all attempts. Perhaps I could achieve my goal through my enemy by striking fairly harshly in turn to destroy all of her charms.

The date I had set for our dinner was the day after Clara had visited me. So, I did not have to wait long and since I had only cancelled my plans with Jenny at the last minute, Flanders arrived alone. I had taken care to instruct him to meet Jenny at my place.

He glanced around my place questioningly and I felt his mistrust return.

"Jenny isn't here yet?" he asked, trying to remain calm.

"No," I said, casually, patting him on the shoulder. "She must have been delayed. But, don't despair. We'll enjoy ourselves while we wait I have an excellent wine that will enhance our patience…"

He accepted the glass with a concerned, closed expression on his face and drank it down.

"Hey!" I shouted. "Do you plan to be drunk when your beauty arrives here to fall into your arms?"

His smile was even tighter, but he was gradually starting to set aside his fears.

"Never!" he said. "Do you think I've focused on my goal for the past month only to cast it aside now that I've attained it?"

"That's good…" I said, approvingly, as I refilled his glass. "Let us drink to your good fortune and the success of your shadowy undertakings."

We both burst into laughter. I stopped abruptly and stared at Flanders with a glacial expression.

"Enough of this nonsense," I said to him. "How and why did you get to know Clara Conway?"

His laughter died in his throat and I watched as the color drained from his face. He glanced around fearfully, looking for an exit.

"There's no point," I said, without blinking. "No door or window in this house can be opened by a human hand."

I observed his panic for a moment. It was exquisite.

"So," I continued. "You were not afraid to speak with the woman you knew to be my mortal enemy, in the hope, no doubt, of continuing your miserable little machinations against me while at the same time trying to sooth me with sweet talk and unctuous smiles?"

"Listen to me Heili..."

His throat was so constricted by fear that he was unable to complete his sentence.

In an icy tone, I observed, "I never called myself Heiligenshtadt. My name is Cagliostro and you knew that. Given the circumstances and knowing of my fame through the centuries, how could you have been so unwitting as to stand up against me? Did you think that your automobiles, your cooling machines and your flying devices would protect you against my vengeance? Were you so vainly stupid that you thought you would defeat me?"

He fell into a chair, his face drenched in sweat.

"You seem to have vaguely realized that you were nothing more than a mediocre small man, too diminished by your vices since you took pains to seek out an ally you believed to be stronger than I am. But I am also taking my revenge on her as well... And don't forget that, even if she had defeated me, you belong to her and your fate would be no better. Also, it is useless to call out to her in your thoughts, as you are doing right now. You are locked in a place from which nothing, neither material objects or thoughts, can escape. And if the impossible happened and she were to fly to your rescue, I must inform you that she would only do so in order to keep you for her research and her evil spells, as a beast whose suffering and death mean nothing."

As I uttered those words, a breath of hot air washed over the room. Flanders and I were being suffocated. I leapt out of the reach of the burning air while Flanders, terrified, threw himself to the ground and rolled about on the carpet.

It only lasted a few seconds and did not recur. But I knew that there must be a breech in the invisible wall I had erected around myself. I did not have the luxury of time to think about that. Flanders had gotten up and was clinging to the wall. I saw his eyes grow wide as he seemed to be looking at something behind me. I turned my head. Seated in an armchair, Clara was staring at us, calmly looking back and forth from one to the other. Her gaze stopped on me and grew hard.

"I thought I had told you I didn't want you to touch this man, since I had reserved him and the girl for myself."

I tried to buy time.

"How did you manage to get to me?" I asked, sounding sheepish.

She smiled and removed her spectacles, which she cleaned carefully with the edge of her black dress.

"You've forgotten a fair number of things," she said, putting her glasses back on. "Don't expect me to list them. All you need to know is that I'm leaving with this man."

I raised my hand, saying "Wait a minute. Wait a minute! I was in the process of working and I would appreciate it if you would leave him with me until I've finished with him."

Without waiting for a response, I left Flanders, frozen with fear, and Clara, jeering, and stepped into the other room, where I picked up an object on which I placed my greatest hopes. It was an oval mirror, made of glass containing one percent gold and polished with iron powder and cobalt oil. Had it been made otherwise, it would have been a simple mirror used to reflect the images of people at a distance. But I had given it infinitely more dangerous properties.

When I returned to the parlor, Clara chuckled when she saw the object I was carrying so carefully.

"I see you're still into nonsense," she said, clasping her hands and looking at me with pity.

I hunched my shoulders, as if I were ashamed of my ignorance and my lack of knowledge.

I stammered, "It's… It's an excellent mirror!"

She started to laugh louder. No doubt she had underestimated me and that was the most serious error she could have made.

Flanders, continued to lean against the wall and was looking back and forth, from Clara to me, with the same expression of fear.

Without hesitating I said, "I assure you, Clara, that I have had some very interesting success with this mirror."

Since I was standing close to her, juggling the mirror from one hand to the other, with a mortified expression on my face, she stood partway up and grabbed it from my hands.

"Let's have a look at this little marvel," she said in a serious tone.

"Look into it for a moment," I said to her. "I do believe you'll be surprised what you see appear in it!"

She gave me a scornful glance then concentrated on the mirror.

Flanders had not moved at all. He was trembling all over, glancing back and forth, like a trapped animal. I stayed there, frozen, hands clasped behind my back, observing Clara. If she managed to determine the true nature of the mirror, she would counterattack immediately and I had no idea how she would do that.

It lasted a minute and suddenly, I heard a deep rumble and the building seemed to shake on its foundations.

Clara moved as if to defend herself but was unable to complete her action. I saw her twist and shrink at an unimaginable speed, as she seemed to be drawn into the mirror. The rumble grew louder. The lights went out. I heard deep cracks form in the walls and the one which Flanders had taken refuge against crumbled with a deafening din. Half of the ceiling fell into the room and I felt my eyes and mouth fill with acrid dust. I fumbled my way over to the chair where Clara had been sitting. It was empty. Looking carefully through the dark, I managed to find the mirror and I leapt through the enormous hole in the wall where Flanders had been, rushing out of the house as it continued to collapse

I saw the archivist running along the road. I paid no attention to him and hurried to examine the mirror in the moonlight.

It was no longer a mirror. It was a sort of somewhat blurry miniature representing Clara sitting in an armchair. My heart leapt madly in my chest. My enemy was now imprisoned in the magic glass. For all eternity this time...

STEVE FLANDERS' ACCOUNT

I will remember the terrifying time I spent in that cursed villa, that I had been asked to purchase for my downfall, for my entire life. In all sincerity, I must say that I did have a hand in that situation. After all, I had summoned that demon Cagliostro in the hope of dispatching Fletcher and keeping Jenny. But I had toyed with powers so far beyond human nature that my natural dissimulation had been insufficient to protect me. That's how I fell into Cagliostro's trap, a sinister meeting attended by someone who had not been invited. The author of *Tragic Philosophies*, still alive after two centuries through some unknown twist in the laws of the universe, had just fought over me with my persecutor for the power to treat me in the same manner he had. The battle between the two powers had freed me, but Cagliostro would never leave me in peace.

I only start my tale from the time at which it took a threatening turn for me, namely the evening I almost lost my life in the villa I mentioned earlier.

I ran so fast and so long to escape from the monstrous battle fought by Clara Conway and Cagliostro, that I fell in the snow and stayed there in a faint. If some obliging passerby had not come to my rescue, I would have died of the cold before the night was over since I would most certainly never have regained consciousness. Yet I was soon warmed in the comfortable taxi that took me home.

While taking the elevator, I heard an indistinct voice murmuring something in my ear. I turned about, looked in all directions. I was alone.

"I'll have to see a doctor," I thought. "This entire situation has been terribly hard on me and if it results in hearing problems, I shouldn't wait to become totally deaf before I seek treatment."

The elevator was ascending gently, smoothly, silently. It was late. I stepped onto the landing, After the light from the elevator vanished behind closed doors and before I pressed the switch for the timed light, I very distinctly heard a hateful voice call me a blackguard.

I found the switch. I turned on the light. I was still alone.

I inserted the key in the lock with a trembling hand. Question: Was Cagliostro already following me or did I need a long rest?

The apartment was cold and empty. I lit the gas stove and made myself a boiling cup of tea before undressing.

I had considered informing the police about the persecutions people were planning to subject me to but, since I could not have told the truth, I decided against that.

As I slipped into bed, I felt a sharp pain in my left foot, as if a sewing needle had been caught in the sheets. That was not impossible since, as a bachelor, I mended my own clothing and had a habit of putting my needles down anywhere, even where I had sewn on a button.

I got up, pulled the covers off and examined the sheets carefully. I did not find a needle. I climbed back into bed, attributing the pain to some spontaneous nervous reaction. Then I felt the same pain in the exact same place a second time. I picked up the first object within reach, my wristwatch as it turned out, and slipped it under the sheets to the exact place where I had been stung, to mark the location.

I got out of bed a second time, examined the sheet and patted it. There was no needle at the spot where I had placed my wrist watch. I finally decided to get back into bed, positioning my legs to avoid the dangerous area. I wasn't exactly pleased about sleeping in a place where there were needles but, since I hadn't found any, there was nothing else to be done about it. When I kept my distance from that spot, I felt no pain. I turned over, trying to get comfortable and placed my wristwatch on the bedside table. It was about a meter from me, but I could hear its tick tock. Since my hearing is excellent and the night was quiet, that did not surprise me.

But when I pulled the cover up over my pillow and I could still hear the tick tock of the watch, I started to find it strange. I lifted my head off the pillow and looked through the darkness in the direction of the watch. I could see the face, which was backlit. The crazy watch was ticking as loudly as a clock. Sleeping was impossible under such conditions. I reached out my hand to grasp the watch and bury it under my pillow to smother its abnormal noise, but I was unable to reach it. I bent over and stretched my arm out to its full length, but my fingers were still too far away. The situation was growing extraordinary. I wanted to clear this matter up. I turned on the light and looked at my watch. I clearly saw it move on the small bedside table, the bracelet moving awkwardly and clumsily like a crab. It reached the edge of the table and fell to the floor. I heard the sound of glass breaking.

I stayed there, dumbfounded, for several seconds, then got out of bed to pick it up. Obviously, the ticking had stopped.

"Blackguard!" repeated the voice I had heard earlier in the elevator.

I turned around and looked in all the corners of the room. I was still alone. How could someone be in my place? I sat down on the edge of the bed, feeling unsettled and discouraged. Nothing was going well. I was experiencing continuous hallucinations. Did Cagliostro have something to do with it? Was it just a series of unsettling jokes? I wanted to chase away the sense of malaise that was washing over me and I headed to the kitchen to drink a large glass of icy water. On my way, I felt an atrocious pain in my left foot, where I thought I had been jabbed by a needle. I stopped, sat down on the carpet and examined my bare foot. I saw nothing. No sign of a wound, no injury. I saw nothing on the carpet either. It was not a cramp, but more like an inner burning, located a small distance under the skin. I stood up. The pain did not return and I walked into the kitchen.

I had barely picked up the glass when it slipped through my fingers and crashed onto the floor tiles. I took care not to walk on the debris since I would have truly injured myself. I swept everything against the wall, planning to throw it into the garbage can. That's when I noticed that my left foot was covered with blood.

Frightened, I raced over to the sink to clean my wounds. Under my fingers, the tap twisted as if it were made of rubber then immediately returned to its initial position. I looked at my foot. There was no sign of blood.

Outside, snow was starting to fall against the windows. In the blinding light of the neon tube that lit the kitchen, I distinctly saw that the snowflakes were red.

This time I was truly frightened. This bloody hallucination had a stranglehold on me. As I considered that thought, I heard a sort of scraping on the tile floor behind me. I spun around. An enormous dog stood motionless halfway into the kitchen. His eyes were bloodshot and his lips were pulled back revealing long, sharp canine teeth. No! If I allowed hallucinations to demoralize me, Cagliostro could simply come and I would let him slit my throat like some bleating lamb.

I walked straight at the image looking at me.

I had barely taken one step when the dog rushed at me with a bestial growl and bit my left thigh. I screamed in fear and pain and, grabbing an immense kitchen knife that was lying near the gas heater, I held it over the beast tearing at my flesh and plunged the sharp blade into its shoulder. It went limp and slumped to the floor.

I stared stupidly at my ravaged, blood covered thigh, at the animal as it trembled convulsively without uttering a sound, at the blade stuck in its shoulder, and at the pool of blood surrounding its curly, black hair. I fell back and struck my head on the floor tiles. I passed out.

When I regained consciousness, the dog was gone and the knife was back in its place near the heater. But my thigh was still torn and bloody and my injury was enormously painful. I felt very weak. I bandaged my wound and decided to get a tetanus shot the next morning. I walked back to my bedroom, leaning against the walls for support. I moaned with each step I took.

"Blackguard!" grated a voice inside my head. I shook myself and clenched my jaws in on effort to overcome my terror.

Cagliostro was starting to play with me like a cat plays with a mouse. Only God alone knew when he would stop and what would be left of me then.

As I entered my bedroom, I jumped back so abruptly that my injured leg collapsed under me and I fell to my knees. I remained there, feeling distraught, torn between suffering and the horror of the new vision that awaited there.

The entire room was filled with a bluish light that seemed to radiate from each object. Jenny was hanging in the middle of the room, swinging gently. Behind my back, the voice spoke again and, for the first time, I recognized it. Cagliostro's voice.

"Murderer!" the voice said. "You killed her! I saw you. I'll tell the police how you caught her. You'll be sentenced to death and executed."

The scent of incense filled the room. I thought I heard a children's choir in the wall, singing a Christmas song.

Holding my thigh, I walked over to the hanging body. I grasped the body by the legs and tried to unhook the wire suspended from the ceiling. But it fell apart against me and melted into a myriad of small, red insects that swept over me from head to foot in the blink of an eye. I rolled about on the floor and they vanished.

I lay there, lying on my belly, holding my face in my hands, for almost an hour. I heard quiet whistles and viscous swarming sounds all around me. Finally, silence fell. My leg felt dead. I chanced a glance around the room and saw that everything had returned to normal.

I got up painfully. I walked over to the window and opened it to breathe in the icy night air. Sweat poured from me. Outside, instead of the usual landscape of walls and rooftops, I saw a furious sea pounding at the foot of the house. Gigantic waves crashed against the wall, shaking the building on its foundations.

A monstrous ship sailed along the horizon. Its shape reminded me of an old-fashioned breast plate. It was heading directly toward me and its silhouette grew larger second by second. Soon, I could make out its armor, dripping with water, shining dully in the moonlight. On each side of the hull, near the railings, immense airplane propellers spun slowly, and everything rose and fell with the waves. It was dizzying. I saw the steel ram extending from its bow plough toward me and through the shrieking wind I heard the choppy rhythm of its engines grow louder and louder.

The vision was so terribly realistic, despite the nightmare atmosphere in which it appeared to me, that I stepped back, expecting to feel the floor vanish from beneath my feet as the house collapsed under the leviathan's blows.

Something touched my on the calves of my legs, stopping my movement. I fell backward for a moment, then stood up, trembling. In front of me, the window was closed, the night was calm and everything in the room looked as it usually did. The light was back on. Nothing remained of my hallucinations. Yet, my leg felt very weak. I looked down at it. The bandage I had wrapped around it was still in place. I peeled one edge back cautiously. The wound was still there, but I was no longer in pain.

I lay back down on my bed and fell into a deep sleep haunted with strange dreams that I recognized, upon waking, as quite different from my hallucinations.

When I woke the next morning, my leg felt so heavy that I quickly removed the bandage to see how the wound was healing. The cause of the injury was beyond comprehension because there was no dog in my home and there could not have been a dog there. Yet the wound did prove that everything that had happened to me the previous evening had not been just a hallucination.

Once I had unwrapped the bandage, I looked at my thigh in terror. The wound was healing. But what an incredible sight! The entire external surface of my thigh was covered with shiny scales. When I ran my hand over the surface, I felt the same cold, viscous sensation one experiences with grabbing a fish at a merchant's stall. It was perfectly horrible.

I went out to head to the library. I was saving the evening to see what had happened to Jenny. Above all, I feared that she had been kidnapped by Cagliostro. But, during the course of the morning, my thoughts grew more self-centered since I had the impression that the readers were staring at my hands. Before noon, I felt that they were looking at my face in disgust. Panicked, I left the library before closing time, overwhelmed by the thought that the hideous transformation of the wound on my thigh could have extended to my entire body and that I now looked like a monster.

At home, unsettled and feverish, I looked at myself in the mirror. It was not obvious. Yet certain pearly reflections, certain wrinkles that crisscrossed on a regular basis, could create an impression of scales. Perhaps my vision wasn't as clear as a result of the transformation of my injury and perhaps it was surprising that others would be aware of it. As far as I was concerned, there was no doubt. My monstrosity appeared clearer and clearer to me with each passing second. I wanted to believe that the light was modifying my features but I had to accept the obvious. My eyes were fixed and bulging, my nose was collapsing and my mouth was growing larger, the corners drooping significantly. Not only did my terrifying transformation prevent me from going to see Jenny, as I had planned, but it also meant I had no desire whatsoever to go out and show my face in the street. I decided to shut myself away at home and dragged a chair over to the mirror.

I made myself a sandwich, since I was starving to death, but I avoided eating in front of the mirror since I did not want to see my teeth. I felt that they were abnormally sharp against my tongue and there were considerably more of them than before.

When I had completed my pitiful meal, I took my clothes off and went to sit in the chair I had placed in front of the mirror. I sat there motionless, observing myself. The scales I had noticed on my thigh when I woke seemed less clear, but my entire body seemed to be coated with a pearly substance and the expression on my face had grown so terrifying that after a few moments I could no longer look myself in the face. I got up from the chair and went to lie down on my bed.

Soon, dizziness overwhelmed me. I felt as if my bed were tossing right and left and I saw the walls spin in a horrifying manner. I closed my eyes. Was I suffering the effect of some illness or was Cagliostro continuing to torture me from a distance?

When I felt my sense of balance grow more stable and my nausea had disappeared, I opened my eyes. A few meters away, Cagliostro was comfortably ensconced in the chair I had placed in front of the mirror. He was observing me with an ironic expression on his face.

I leapt up and glanced sidewise at the door to the bedroom.

"No!" he said in a smooth voice. "You know full well that you belong to me. Have you been enjoying the little games we've been playing?"

I did not respond but continued to glance furtively at the door, evaluating the distance that separated me from it and trying to determine how my torturer would react if I tried to flee.

"I wouldn't react at all," he said, replying to my thought as if reading my mind. "You would simply be stopped since the door would not open. Everywhere I go, doors never open, either for my own security or to prevent my guests from leaving me."

I remained silent. Cagliostro looked at me critically.

"You'd better get dressed," he said. "You're going to have a visitor."

My fear grew. What sinister trick did he have up his sleeve for me... I would find out soon enough. I had barely finished dressing, under Cagliostro's scornful eye, when the doorbell rang.

"Be quick! Open the door!" he said, pounding on the arm of the chair.

Fear of what I was about to see on the other side of the door grew even stronger. I stepped back and yelled," Open it yourself!"

He leaned forward and I saw his eyes blaze.

"How dare you!" he roared.

Then he relaxed, leaned back against the chair and burst into laughter. I stood there, shivering, as the doorbell rang again.

He stopped laughing abruptly and stared at me. That was enough. Like a robot, I marched into the front hall. I walked over to the door, hesitated a second, then pulled it open quickly. On the doorstep stood my wife, who had been dead ten years, staring at me with glassy eyes.

I backed away slowly, my chest caught in a vise. She moved ahead immediately, as if bound to me by some invisible thread. I took three quick steps back, reaching my hands out in front of me to protect myself. She immediately slid toward me, without moving, so that the distance between us did not grow. I suddenly struck the wall at the back of the vestibule. She stopped in the light floating out of my bedroom. I heard a new burst of laughter from that room. I slumped in the corner of the wall and closed my eyes. All that I had experienced over the past 48 hours, perhaps even everything that had happened since I had read *Tragic Philosophies* and dragged Crawson along in my wake, had to be a nightmare.

I opened my eyes. She walked over to me. I pressed my back against the wall. She moved even closer to me. I felt her body against mine. I felt her icy arms wrap around my neck. Her eyes were like those black pools you imagine people drown in... I allowed myself to slip to the floor and lost consciousness.

The Christmas music I had heard the previous day resonated nearby. At the same time, the scent of incense floated around me. I opened my eyes. I was lying on my back and immense vaults lit by a multitude of candles, floated overhead, at dizzying heights. Deafening music burst out all around me. I could hear trumpet bursts, the deep base voices of choirs... I rolled violently onto my side. I was lying on a raised surface from which I looked down on an immense crowd packed into the confines of a gigantic nave. Nearby, stood a man wearing a gold-embroidered linen robe. His hands were clasped and his head was bowed. I could hear the notes of the Stabat mater.

I tried to get up and climb down from the sort of marble table on which I was lying, but that was impossible. All I could do was scream and writhe in despair. The strange priest who was officiating, raised his clasped hands over his head and started to chant odd words that sounded to me like Sanskrit. I could only make out bits and pieces since everything else was overwhelmed by the music echoing off the vaulted ceiling.

Soon, other men dressed in white, no doubt priests, cut through the crowd of followers and approached the officiant. They exchanged a few quick words in another language and then they grabbed me by my hands and feet. They carried me thorough the church and I did not resist. As I was carried toward the door, I caught glimpses of what looked like byzantine frescoes decorating the walls. Their beauty filled me with joy despite the violent manner in which I was being treated.

Outside, it was very cold. I was placed in a spacious, comfortable car and I fell in a sleep filled with dreams. At that point I could no longer tell the difference between hallucinations and dreams, as I did in the past and as I do now. The dreams I had while in the car were so complex and so interwoven with the events that had preceded my sleep that I cannot separate them. Perhaps I will be able to in the future.

In any case, when I woke, I found myself in a proper bed and in a room that was not mine. I glanced about at the bright, white walls. There was a small metal table near the head of the bed and, when I turned my head, I saw a man dressed in white sitting on a chair on the other side of the bed. He seemed to be watching me.

"Father," I said, "Father, please tell me where I am. I thank the Church for taking care of me, but I assure you that I am not ill and I do not want to inconvenience you."

He made a peaceful motion as if advising me to rest. He got up and left the room. He locked the door behind himself.

Terror filled me at the thought of being alone. What if Cagliostro were to come back and start torturing me again! In this isolated room, with the door closed, with the window covered with thick bars, I would be entirely at his mercy and I could never hope to be rescued by anyone.

I tried to get up again. It was only then that I understood why I did not feel perfectly comfortable. My arms were bound, crossed behind my back in a piece of clothing made of solid fabric with the ends of the sleeves tied across my chest.

I lay back down, feeling calmer. The priests were taking care of me. They had certainly used my position and the jacket to create a ritual barrier between me and my torturer. I felt very grateful to them and fell asleep again.

When I awoke, I was still alone. I waited patiently for someone to take care of me and soon I heard the key turn in the lock. Another priest came in and I thanked him for the protection he gave me. I explained to him that I fully trusted the effectiveness of the clothing I had been given. He smiled and prepared to remove it. Once again overcome by fear, I asked if he were certain that I was in no danger... He reassured me.

As soon as my hands were free, I asked for paper and a pen.

"I want you to know everything about me," I said. "I intend to transcribe my story."

He gave me what I wanted.

It's done. Someone must come to see me today. I'm waiting, without a concern!

JENNY'S ACCOUNT

I waited 24 hours after Fletcher's disappearance to notify the police. During that time, Steve came and gave me an explanation for that absence that was plausible, yet painful to accept.

I did not understand how Fletcher, who had always seemed to love me, or at least care for me deeply, could have suddenly left me to go back to London, where he had nothing to do. However, I did allow Steve to console me and he did not seem to want to replace Fletcher, just give me a little comfort. He remained distant enough that I allowed him to come and see me.

After a few days he came to see me accompanied by an extremely strange friend who made me feel terribly afraid for the first time. The day before he disappeared, Fletcher had told me about his adventure in the library and had provided a rough description of the fantastic character he had encountered. Steve's friend fit that description so closely I had no doubt it was the same person.

But, at the end of the first interview, my conviction was shaken. A little voice in my heads kept telling me it could not be Ulrich von Heiligenshtadt... and another fact cancelled my initial impression, reassuring me, making me feel calm and detached in a way I had never felt before.

I had a meeting with the man and he was so courteous I felt I was dealing with an exceptional person. But the dinner he offered to organize for Steve and me did not take place. The evening I was supposed to go, I felt such a strong desire to stay home that I could not set foot outside. I experienced a curious determination, as if it came from outside me. But the calmness I mentioned earlier prevented me from growing concerned, like pain that is annihilated by anesthesia.

That's when Steve stopped his visits.

I was left to my own devices for two days and only the important work I was doing to arrange decorative accessories in the store front window washed away a portion of the bitter regret Fletch's absence filled me with.

Saturday came and, with it, a long empty day. In ordinary times, and if I had been my usual cheerful self, I would have used my free hours well, but my sorrow and my curious detachment from reality drove me to hunker down at home, to read or dream about the happy days I had spent at Fletch's side.

I was just finishing my morning ablutions when the doorbell rang. The first thought that came to my mind was that Steve had news about Fletch and had come to share it with me.

I ran a comb through my hair and went to open the door. It was just some gas company employee come to read the meter. He spoke only a few words to me, but his tone made something in my memory click. I knew that low voice, that accent...

After the employee left, I searched through my mind for a moment. Good grief! It was the voice of Steve's friend, the friend I still could not make myself refer to as Heiligenshtadt, although everything inside me convinced me that it was that man.

I set to work on washing a large load of clothing since I had washed nothing for several days and dirty laundry was piling up. I was interrupted by another ring of the doorbell. This time it had to be Steve.

It was another employee. From the water company, this time. While the first employee had been short and quite corpulent, this one was tall and thin.

But just as he said, "Is Mr. Crawson, here? I've come to read the meter..." shivers ran up and down my back. It was the same voice.

Once he left, I sat down at a kitchen chair, in front of my interrupted laundry. What did the strange similarity of the voices of such disparate individuals mean? And why did their voices sound just like that of... of Steve's friend, the friend whose name he had not given me, even when he had introduced us to one another... I do believe he had said, "He's a friend" and nothing else.

If he had been the man Fletch had met, Steve would have known that since they had seen him together. The fact that he had not given me the man's name must mean that they both had plans that should concern me. As for the rest, I was just starting to grasp some poorly defined danger... That fear coincided with a sort of liberation, a bit like the disappearance of a restriction someone had placed on my sense of judgement...

How could I have remained so blind to the identity of Steve's friend for so long? It now seemed clear to me that the friend was Heiligenshtadt. Flanders' behavior suddenly seemed so ambiguous that I immediately decided they were working together on some very suspicious undertaking.

The doorbell rang again.

This time, when I headed for the door, I walked slowly. I felt that I looked very pale. I no longer imagined that I would see Flanders... I opened after hesitating for a long time, as the bell rang a third time.

A poorly dressed man stood on the landing, He handed me a paper without saying a word. I glanced at it and quickly read:

"The French Association of Deaf-Mutes invites you to an exhibit of art works created by deaf-mute artists and workers for the benefit of..."

I looked back up at the man, who smiled and made some gestures with his fingers. I thanked him and closed the door, keeping the paper. With my ear against the door, I heard him walk slowly down the stairs. Then his footsteps melted into the silence.

A deaf-mute, after two men with the same voice... What did that strange coincidence mean? I had no doubt at all that if this third visitor had had a voice, it too would have been Heiligenshtadt's...

No sooner had that thought entered my head then I realized how absurd it was. Here I was starting to worry more about a mute man than about a man who spoke in the voice of that mysterious German... In fact, the thought I had considered absurd did have a significance. It revealed my fear that, in an envelope that was different each time, it was always Heiligenshtadt who was visiting me.

The doorbell rang again, but I did not open the door. There were far too many visitors this morning... and I knew whose voice I would hear...

I stood frozen behind the door, holding my breath. The doorbell rang again and I heard rustling on the floor. Looking down, I saw an envelope being slipped under the floor. I heard footsteps walking down the stairs and stood there, motionless, until they disappeared. Only then did I bend down to pick up the envelope.

It was addressed to me in Steve's handwriting. I opened it, took out a small piece of paper on which a few words were written:

"I don't have time to tell you why I left Paris. Just know that I was in danger and that, where I am going, I have nothing to fear. Can you come and join me? I have news of Crawson, but I can't send it to you for reasons I will clarify in person."

This was followed by an address in Orléans. What the devil had Flanders gone to do in Orléans and what danger threatened him in Paris? It was his handwriting but I feared it hid some trap. Either he had organized things with Flanders himself, or the letter had been written under some threat. Yet the promise of receiving news about Fletch made my heart race and I had to force myself to keep from throwing on my clothes and rushing immediately to the Austerlitz station.

I went slowly back to my exasperating laundry, that was far from over, as long as the day continued to pass with the same hustle and bustle with which it had started.

What should I do? Should I go to Orlans and run the risk of falling into a trap? Should I stay in Paris and refuse to learn what happened to Fletch?

I started pacing up and down and nervously lit a cigarette. I would have given anything to know if there was some sort of connection between this worrisome meeting with a man who had hidden the truth from me and the unlikely coincidence of the sound of the voice I had heard... Yet, I could learn a lot from the meeting with Flanders... Either he would tell me the truth about Fletch's departure for England—and there was no reason in that case to suspect the news he claimed to possess— or he had lied and was involved in some plot that put

Fletch in danger... In that case, going courageously to the address would give me an opportunity to conduct a little investigation and tear the truth from Flanders by force in place of a new lie.

After all, it might be possible to stop him if I took the precaution of using Fletcher's revolver, which was in the drawer of his desk...

I did not waste much time considering the pros and cons. I dressed quickly, picked up some cash and slipped everything into the pocket of my coat.

When I walked past the concierge's office, I saw him sorting mail.

"Someone brought the mail up to me..." I said. "I couldn't open the door. I was taking my bath. Was it you?"

"No," he replied. "And I didn't see anyone go up."

It was Heiligenshtadt's voice.

I raced off as if the devil were at my heels. It was a done deal. Anyone who spoke to me did so with the German's voice. Even if he were some sort of sorcerer, I felt it was much more likely to attribute my impressions to myself... to some sort of auditory obsession... than to suppose that he embodied everyone I met. Such an obsession was already strange enough on its own and I had no need to search for even more twisted hypotheses... such as supposing that the concierge had taken on Heiligenshtadt's personality for a brief moment.

At the train station, I avoided talking with the employees. I was afraid of the voice I would hear. If I continued to hear that tone from all mouths, I would start wondering if such hallucinations were not signs of the early stages of madness.

I settled for reading the departures board to determine when and where I could catch the first train for Orléans.

It was 11:31, on Track 10. I had 13 minutes to wait. That seemed like a bad sign to me.

A train stood on Track 10; it was as empty as if it had been on a siding. I found that surprising since, even during periods when there are few travelers, there are always a few in any given train.

"In thirteen minutes..." I thought, somewhat philosophically. "In thirteen minutes, dozens of people may arrive...." And I went off to purchase a magazine I didn't even bother leafing through.

Twelve minutes later, I climbed into an empty compartment. The passenger car in which the compartment was located was completely empty. When the train set off, I imagined, as a way to comfort myself, that passengers had taken their seats in other cars... But deep down, I was convinced that, apart from the employees, there was no one but me on the train.

I forced myself to smile and said out loud, "They've assigned a special train to me..."

But my heart wasn't in it. My concerns about the appointment in Orléans and the extraordinary atmosphere in the passenger-free train were too troubling. I hunkered down in a seat on the corridor side of the compartment to avoid getting my face covered with soot as always happens when you sit near a window. Then I opened the magazine. I exclaimed in fright. The first page carried a photo of a laughing Heiligenshtadt.

After throwing the strange magazine out the window, I realized I didn't have the courage to remain seated in the compartment. The solitude weighed heavily on me and, apart from the strange concerns that assaulted me, I trembled at the thought of being attacked by a passenger, the only one with me in the entire train.

I found the presence of Fletch's revolver in my pocket reassuring... but if someone did attack me and I had to kill him to save my life, when the train stopped how would I prove that I had legitimately defended myself? And how would I explain the presence of a weapon in my pocket when I had no permit to carry weapons?

I set out and moved through the gangway connection to the next car, which was just as deserted as mine was. I interrupted my exploration and bent down to look out through a window.

We were already out in the countryside even though the train had barely been on its way for ten minutes. It was travelling so rapidly that I could barely make out the trees and the houses as they raced past. That too was not normal. I was starting to regret boarding the train which, while it looked every bit as ordinary as all the others, seemed to come straight out of some nightmare.

I continued on my way. The sight of the countryside racing past at an alarming speed discouraged me from looking out any other windows.

When I had lowered the window to look out, my hands got covered with soot. I walked over to the washroom, intending to wash my hands. I took a step back, feeling strangely afraid and hopeful at the same time. Just above the door handle, the sign said "occupied".

So, I wasn't alone. I found that definitely comforting. But I had not abandoned the idea of washing my hands. I headed for the other end of the car.

The same word was displayed above the door handle. The impression of comfort vanished. Shivering, despite myself, I headed into the next car. Same thing.

Once again, the sign on the door at the other end of the car was the same.

Panicked, I grabbed my revolver in my pocket and knocked on the door. I did not know if the vibrations caused by my blows had caused the latch inside to jump but, as I heard a dry click, I saw the word "Vacant" appear.

After a long pause, I shouted, "Is someone there?"

No one replied. I decided to open the door. The washroom was empty. I washed my hands and was starting to dry them on the towel when, as the train bumped over an uneven switch, the door closed and the latch dropped. I cried out in fear although, under other circumstances, I would not even have grimaced in annoyance.

The latch resisted. I was trapped in a washroom on a deserted train. I started to call for help and looked about for the alarm button. There was no alarm button in the washroom. Just then the train slowed and came to a stop. Through the dirty glass, I heard the hubbub of a large station and a loudspeaker announcing, "Chartres... Chartres... Passengers for..."

I banged on the window, hoping that an employee passing by on the platform would hear me... In vain.

It was only when the train set off again that I thought of using the butt of my revolver to break the window. But by the time I had broken an area large enough to put my head through and call out, the end of the platform had already disappeared behind me and the train was returning to its infernal speed through a city that vanished like a dream, making way for a foggy, monotonous countryside.

I attacked the door again, weeping with anger and fear. Footsteps shook the metal floor on the other side of the door and I heard the sound of a key. I feared what would happen when the door opened. I huddled against the metal wall, staring at the door in fear.

It opened.

In the frame, I saw an inspector, his bag over his shoulder.

"These locks block sometimes," he said. "Do you have your ticket?"

He too spoke in Heiligenshtadt's voice. I handed him my ticket. He looked at it, smiling enigmatically and asked me a question that made me shiver.

"Why did you take a *return* ticket?"

I stammered some sort of excuse. He handed the ticket back to me and turned away. By the time I stepped out of the washroom, he had stepped into the gangway connection... And by the time I stepped into it in turn he had vanished.

The train continued at its breakneck pace. Fear never left me. I even doubted that it had stopped at Chartres. Broken by fatigue and fear, I collapsed on the first bench I saw and fell asleep.

When I woke, everything was dark around me, except for the bluish rectangle of the window in the compartment. Night had fallen, but none of the lights had turned on. I was in an empty, dark train that was racing like lightning through the night. At the speed it was travelling, I must have already passed Orléans... I might even have travelled clear across France... if, for that matter, I was still on Earth.

I was starting to have doubts. Panick overwhelmed me. I fumbled around, looking for an alarm, found it, and pulled on it fully believing that nothing would happen.

A long scream rang out and the train started to slow. After a minute, it stopped. I had no intention of waiting for someone to come and ask me what was going on. I climbed down from the car and ran through a muddy meadow that ran along the track. I heard a loud noise behind me. I turned around, dumbfounded. The train was starting to roll and the red lights on the back of the last car were vanishing in the night.

I continued to race ahead, hoping to find a road at some point that would take me to a house. But the tilled field seemed to extend to the horizon. Yet, I did find a small path that I took. It led me to a sort of wide trail. The moonlight revealed that the unevenness of the ground had been caused by deep footprints created by horses' hooves and by immense ruts.

I walked for a very long time without seeing a single house. Finally, above the tree tops, I saw a tall, steep roof, flanked a tower.

At the same time, a hoarse voice called out from behind a bush, "Who goes there?"

I stopped, trembling. A dark silhouette appeared on the road. It walked toward me, carrying a lamp. It was a tall, broad man wearing tight-fitting pants tucked into very tall boots that flared at the top. He was wearing a tight coat and a three-cornered hat. A sword hung from his belt. In his free hand, he carried an old-fashioned rifle.

"Miss Jenny de Serenzac!" he shouted respectfully. "What are you doing outside at this time when you've just barely been rescued from the Prince of Wurtemberg and the mercenaries are still in the woods!

I tried to tell him that I did not understand what he meant. But I found myself dumbfounded when I hear him say, "Come now, Captain, don't let fear get any more of a grasp on you than I do or the margrave, my adoptive father, will have a very poor opinion of you..."

I had barely finished uttering those words when everything blurred in front of my eyes. The man with the lamp vanished as if he had been made of mist, the road became smooth and I could no longer see the sky. Dizzy, I supported myself on an object moving within reach and, heard, at the same time, an enormous racket and an indignant voice shouting, "The bottles! The bottles! Be careful, Miss! You're going to break everything!"

I glanced soundlessly around me. I had grabbed a small cart loaded with bottles of beer and soda, being pushed by a man through a hall filled with people carrying suitcases. My glance fell on a large clock, hands showing 11:18. I murmured an apology to the man pushing the cart and turned away. The platforms stood in a line in front of me, trains departing. The closest departure board read: "Track 10. Orléans – 11:31."

Had I dreamed everything? I threw my ticket for Orléans on the ground and headed unsteadily for the exit. There I was asked to provide a ticket, any kind of ticket. I returned to the place where I had thrown down my ticket and found it there, blackened by a footstep.

When I presented it to the employee, he observed, "But this ticket has not been used! You're not leaving?"

"No!" I replied. "I'm staying."

I left immediately. This man too was speaking with the German's voice. It was quite real and my dream was continuing on.

"Go to the ticket booth to get a refund," he said. "Hurry up! They won't give you your money back once the train has departed."

At the ticket booth, they assured me, still in the same voice, that they would have given me a refund even if the train had departed. I didn't care. My mind was filled with an idea much more important than getting a refund for the ticket...

As I left the station, I caught a taxi. The state of partial madness in which I had been evolving since the morning had taken, with my most recent encounter—the man with the three-cornered hat—had taken a form which I intuitively knew was dangerous. I had recognized the period and the place where the *Tragic Philosophies* had taken place, based on what Fletch had described to me, and suddenly finding myself entangled with the plot of the book had turned on a sort of red light in my mind. Had Heiligenshtadt... If he had stepped out of the book... had he been trying to draw someone into it? And Fletch... where actually was he?

I climbed out of the taxi in front of the library. I had to be quick about it. The library was closed between noon and one o'clock, which meant that Steve—or his replacement—would be back at 12:45. I had thirty minutes to complete my task.

No one noticed me walk into the library. The few passersby in the place were rushing off to their lunches.

Fletch had told me how surprised he was when he found the doors to the library unlocked. No doubt Flanders was no model employee... But if he was not at his post, perhaps his replacement was more diligent... Yet, the large door opened easily.

But when I climbed the stairs and pushed on the door to the reading room, the same could not be said. I stayed there, undecided, pacing back and forth, thinking I heard footsteps climbing up the steps. There was nothing I could do. This time, the obstacle facing me was insurmountable. I desperately sought a solution and found nothing. At the same time, I had an acute sense of the time passing. In 20 minutes, my project would be reduced to nothing.

I started to pace back and forth and if the expression on my face had not been twisted by anxiety and despair, anyone seeing me would have thought that I was just a very regular reader impatiently waiting for the reading room to open.

I wasted a full ten minutes as my nervousness grew. As time passed, I convinced myself more and more that Heiligenshtadt had tried, in some way or another, to trap me in the book Fletcher had mentioned to me. His attempt had failed but I had had enough time during my train trip and my flight through the muddy countryside— that had left no trace other than that of a simple dream in my mind—to appreciate the hell I had briefly encountered. I most certainly did not want to find myself there again, on a permanent basis. I preferred to kill myself.

Kill myself? But I had a revolver in my pocket! Why didn't I shoot the lock? Of course, that would have produced a terrible racket... But, after all, I was alone in a large building with thick walls and there was little to no chance that anyone in the street would have heard a gunshot...

I positioned myself a meter away from the door, stretched my arm out, aimed carefully... If I missed the lock from this distance, I would deserve everything that would follow. I pressed on the trigger.

As I had expected, the racket the shot made in the large staircase was terrifying. I remained there, frozen, eyes rivetted on the empty stairs, expecting to see a huge crowd surge, at any moment, from the street.

But nothing happened. I turned to look at the door. The lock hung there, partially broken, and the door stood open two centimeters.

I pushed it quickly and entered the reading room, glancing at my watch. I had barely ten minutes left. I wasted one minute wondering what would have happened to the revolver and the watch in the world Heiligenshtadt had tried to drag me into... No doubt, they would have simply disappeared if I had truly entered that world.

The door to the closed stacks opened the same way the one to the reading room had, following a deafening detonation that echoed throughout the large deserted room. I walked through a scent of powder that would have probably given men thoughts of battle while it only made me cough.

I had eight minutes left before the librarian would enter the room and sound the alert. During those eight minutes, I had to get the *Tragic Philosophies*, go down to the basement Fletch had mentioned to me, and burn the book.

I would not have needed all that time if I had known how to find what I was looking for. But the closed stacks had an overwhelming number of books and it was mad to think I would be able to locate one specific book among them all. I rushed over to the card catalogue and found the name "Conway". There were at least fifteen people named Conway who had written something and I rifled quickly through all the cards. Finally, I found "Clara Conway". The card indicated the title of the fatal book. I still had four minutes.

After noting the call number for the book, I raced over to the corresponding shelf. It took me another two minutes to locate the bin marked S and the number... the number was missing. *Tragic Philosophies* was not in the closed stacks.

I spun my heels for a good minute, not knowing what to do, reading the titles at random. The letters on the spines of the books danced so wildly I could not make out their meaning. I stared at my watch, hypnotized. It read a quarter to one. My wrist twitched convulsively and I was unable to stop it.

From the stairs an indignant exclamation rang out. Either the librarian or a reader had to be standing in front of the door I had forced open. I was trapped and I had failed.

Before rushing out of the closed stacks, I glanced back at the small desk on which the boxes filled with cards stood in rows. I saw a large book I had not noticed before because I had used it to support the paper on which I had written the call number.

The title was printed on the spine along with the author's name. Shouting with joy, I rushed toward the desk, grabbed the heavy book, and leapt through the door to the reading room. On my way, I jostled a man who tried to grab me by the arm. I freed myself roughly, kicking his legs, and raced through the second door. From the landing, I rushed into the stairs and it was only a miracle that I did not fall.

On the ground floor, a man and a woman talking in the lobby stopped, and stared at me with dumbfounded expressions. Paying them no attention, I ran to the door of the cellar. On the second floor, the man I had jostled in the reading, had set out to pursue me, yelling.

The door to the basement opened without me having to shoot it and a stone staircase stretched before me. I rushed into it and eventually found myself in the section of the basement reserved for the heating system. The door to that room remained open, no doubt left that way by the man responsible for loading the furnace.

I looked at the boiler. Standing in front of it, arms crossed, Heiligenshtadt forbid me to approach.

I stopped suddenly, struggling to catch my breath. I watched the man in black walk overhead, as he calmly observed, "These people bore us, don't you agree?"

He had barely uttered the last word when I heard something fall in the stone staircase. I turned around and saw two men fall onto the last step. They remained motionless there.

"So," he continued, "You decided to burn this work filled with genius?"

I remained silent, clutching the book to my chest, my heart pounding. He uncrossed his arms, clasped his hands behind his back and started to pace about, as if he were in some parlor. I was seized by a terrible desire to leap toward the boiler, when he was farthest from it... But I would still have to open the grate, using an iron rod and I had no chance of doing that before he could grab the book from my hands.

He stopped and looked at me. He seemed undecided.

"That might be a solution..." he said, pensively.

I couldn't believe my ears.

He continued, 'You've demonstrated a certain amount of initiative and stubbornness. Considering that, I wonder..."

He stopped talking and went back to pacing, muttering under his breath, "I'm tired of Frida. How could I have ever considered, for a single moment, calling her back to me since I have so much to do in this new century? At the same time, she has suffered enough to deserve eternal rest."

He spoke to me without any animosity, saying, "But what makes you think that you will attain your goal by burning the only copy?"

My goal! But if he wasn't trying to chain me to the book, I no longer had any goal!

He must be reading my thoughts since he continued, saying, "Are you no longer interested in Crawson?"

Good grief! My eyes were opened for the first time! Fletch had suffered the same fate I had feared for myself...

"Whatever..." he added. "If the destruction of a single copy is effective... like a symbol, we will see our friend return to us... and that will give me information about Frida's fate. As for myself, I have nothing to fear since I'm no longer part of the book."

He walked over to me and took the book from my hands. Dumbfounded, I watched him walk over to the fireplace and open the grate. He turned to look at me and smiled as he said, "I have great plans for this century," he said. "I prefer to keep both of you... You'll be excellent instruments in my hands, once I've stripped you of your personalities."

He turned to the open iron grate and threw the book into the flames... But he barely had time to stand back up when he dropped like a rock to the cement floor.

I approached, frightened, His body had disappeared. I was alone in the basement, standing in front of the fireplace, where the diabolical book burned.

Moans, then curses, followed by the sound of running footsteps came from the stairs to the basement. I turned around. Two men, followed by a woman, were running toward me, shouting in anger. Other people were walking down the stairs, talking animatedly. I let them take me away without resisting.

CONCLUSIONS

"To sum it all up," the doctor started to say. "Here's my version of what happened…"

Fletcher Crawson and Jenny Serenzac settled back into the easy chairs where they sat. These chairs were close enough to one another that they could hold hands while the psychiatrist spoke.

They had been treated at the same hospital as Flanders, but had been discharged relatively quickly while the archivist might well never recover his wits. Before doing anything else, they had had the bans read for their upcoming marriage. And they had made an appointment with the doctor who had treated them in the hospital to discuss their adventure at his home and not in an institutional setting. They had been given a few opinions already, but the explanations, too fragmentary, had not satisfied them.

The matter of the doors that had been shot open with a revolver had resulted in Jenny being brought before a court, but the psychiatrist's testimony had cleared her from all responsibility and, although she had been declared fully healed, he had admitted that her action, at the time she had taken it, revealed a mental state for which she could not be blamed. She had been sentenced to simply repair the damage caused.

"First, of all," the doctor continued, "The events that took you to the hospital took place within a group whose members shared a racial affinity since all three of you are of English descent. It is well known that, in terms of character, most English people manifest a certain duality in which tendencies toward the concrete and practical efficiency stand in opposition to an emotional backdrop with a certain mystique that does not reject the marvelous. This is merely a starting argument but in a matter as troubling as this one, nothing must be neglected."

Jenny and Fletcher nodded and smiled.

"Now, let's take a look at Flanders' case, which seems to be by far the most interesting. Here we have a man who has been living alone for ten years, whose physical advantages are mediocre as a result of his age, and who is far too corpulent for his height. Yet his imagination is very fertile when it comes to erotic matters. Two factors played a role in the development of his psychoses: an intense physical attraction to you, young lady, resulting in a guilt complex and blind faith in the mediumistic. It was a short step from there to trying to use occult sciences to attain his goal. At that point, the psychosis had not developed as yet, but the soil was fertile.

"In all likelihood the disease started with an obsessive desire to conquer you, Miss Serenzac, and it gradually transformed into a powerful desire that was indistinctly applied.

"At the second stage, in Flanders' subconscious, this powerful desire came into conflict with the guilt complex created by his desire for you. All in all, two mental states resulting from a third, battled one another, which caused the patient, whose self-censorship was very violent, to split his personality in two."

Crawson raised his hand in protest.

"Wait, wait," said the psychiatrist. "Then we saw the appearance, inside Mr. Flanders, of a sort of mental cyst that grew monstrously large and fast, namely the Cagliostro-ego."

"Or the Heiligenshtadt-ego..." added Crawson.

"No, no, not yet. The Heiligenshtadt-ego came after, because it is a complication, a re-working of the first. What are the relationships between these two personalities, each of which contains elements of the personality of the healthy Flanders? Heiligenshtadt's pride, Flanders' hypocrisy. Well, it's quite simple. The Cagliostro-ego enslaved the Flanders-ego, using a mechanism of self-punishment resulting directly from the guilt complex. That's the third stage of the illness, which you got involved in... And the fourth and final stage, the stage Flanders is currently in and which is described in the manuscript which he signed with his real name, is characterized by the resorption of the parasite ego and the flourishing of the hallucinatory persecution delirium."

Jenny nodded and asked, "And how do you view our case?"

"It's fairly similar for both of you, although you have been treated for different symptoms. You, young lady, arrived at the hospital as a result of antisocial behavior, for which the causes had already disappeared by the time of your arrest. As for you Mr. Crawson, you came to visit Flanders on your own and as a result of the comments you made, combined with signs of melancholic depression we decided to keep you for a few days..."

"But you said our cases were similar?" Jenny asked.

"I'm getting to that. The accounts each of you provided of your hallucinations were crosschecked with Flanders' two manuscripts—the one he penned under the name Ulrich Von Heiligenshtadt, which was found at his home, and the one he wrote at the hospital under his own name, Flanders."

"But how do you know the first one was written by Flanders?" Crawson protested

"The handwriting is the same," replied the psychiatrist. "It's Flanders' handwriting. We compared the four accounts based on the examinations and tests we subjected all three of you to and found something that is not rare in medical literature: the extension of the patient's hallucinatory delirium outside himself and its appearance in those he is involved with. In general, this only occurs within a single family. For example, the mother's delusion of persecution becomes so convincing that those around her take part in it and retaliate against innocent neighbors. In your case, the contagion occurred at a speed that is rarely seen and you took part in Flanders' delusion in a deep yet fortunately brief manner."

Fletcher and Jenny remained unconvinced...

Jenny asked, "But then, supposing that everything took place only in our imaginations, how long did our...madness last? And what were we really doing all that time?"

The psychiatrist frowned and replied, "That point isn't quite clear. You were probably only ill for a short time, for just a few days: an acute psychotic episode..."

He glanced at them sideways and continued, "And I can't be certain no trace will be left since you both seem fairly close to believing in the reality of your delusion."

"We don't believe in anything," said Crawson in a positive tone. "We are totally at a loss. That's why we've asked you for your opinion... in an effort to try and make our own."

"But what did we do when we were in that... state?" asked Jenny, clinging to her idea.

The psychiatrist opened his arms, palms up, saying "That's impossible to know. The police report only indicates that your apartment was empty for four days. But there is nothing to prove that you were not already ill before your absence. And as for knowing where you went..."

Fletcher and Jenny exchanged a glance...

"So..." Jenny continued, "Everything we saw was just hallucinations? Then how do you account for the fact that, during what you refer to as my delusion, I chose between what I saw and heard, reporting certain impressions as hallucinations—like Heiligenshtadt's voice coming from everyone's mouths—and others as true perceptions... such as Heiligenshtadt's vision?"

"Ha, ha, ha," the psychiatrist said, smiling. "For a decorative artist, you use language that is quite scientific."

"That's because, I've done a lot of reading on the matter since I got better and Fletch helped me understand..." Jenny replied, smiling.

"Well, that's part of the nature of your delusion," explained the doctor. "The fact that you saw Heiligenshtadt was hallucinosis, namely a hallucination that is considered true and that you rejected halfway, by treating it as a hallucination and attributing the responsibility for it to Heiligenshtadt. You were going around in circles."

"Hmmm..." said Jenny.

"Yes..." murmured Fletcher, thoughtfully. "That was what must have happened to me as well.... Considering your interpretation, of course. I do admit that I accept part of your opinion, but there is one question I would like to ask. Did they find out where Flanders got enough money to buy a villa?"

The psychiatrist shook his head, looking embarrassed.

"And did they determine what caused the villa to collapse?" Fletcher added.

The doctor shrugged, and replied reluctantly, "An architectural defect, no doubt.

"And how do you account for the fact that, in the ruins of the house, they found an odd little portrait that seems to have been painted inside a mirror?"

The doctor looked uncomfortable, as he replied, "Flanders must have found that in some antique shop... He must have paid a great deal for it. I have never seen anything like it in my life..."

"Yes," replied Fletcher. As for that file in the library that lists the author and the title of a book that cannot be found..."

Lacking conviction, the psychiatrist replied with a tight smile, "Books do get lost in libraries, Mr. Crawson...".

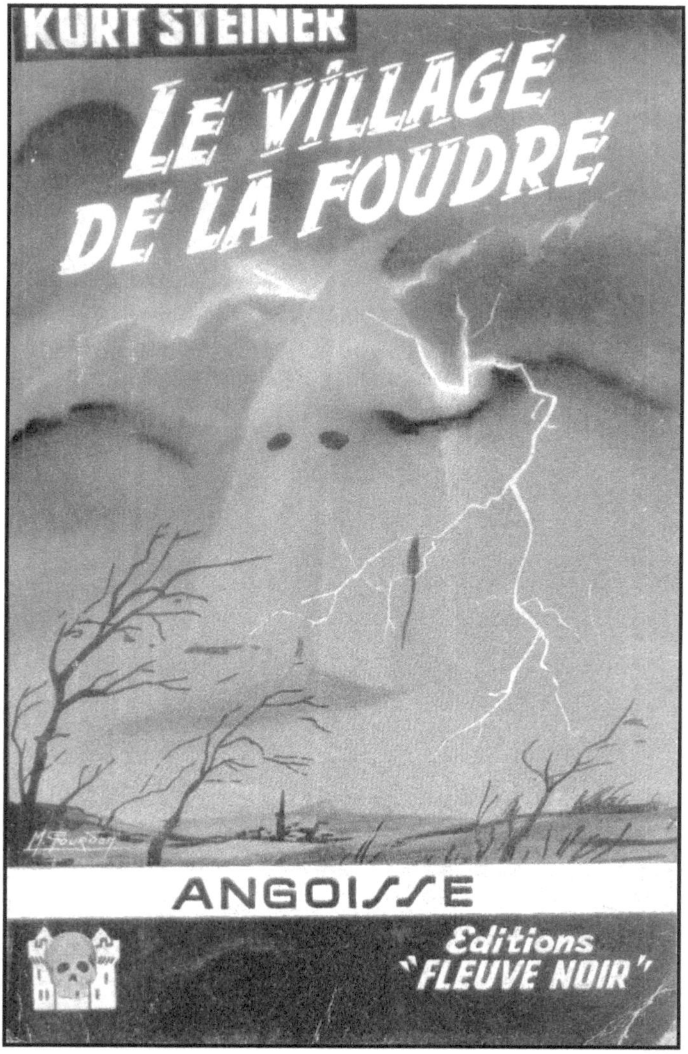
KURT STEINER
LE VILLAGE DE LA FOUDRE
ANGOISSE
Editions "FLEUVE NOIR"

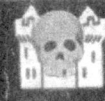

THE VILLAGE OF LEPERS

"Human emotion has a power of influencing
or saturating inanimate nature."
Robert Hugh Benson

CHAPTER I

Among the huddled masses of trees and rocks, the steep road that runs from Olmeto to Mammola seemed to secrete its own light, drawing a pale, scar-like furrow. Night had fallen without bringing coolness. The irritating chirping of the grasshoppers had dropped a notch or so. The oppressed countryside was slipping from vague drowsiness into heavy numbness.

Mario regretted having wandered into this wild, unfamiliar territory so late in the day. His troubles were already starting. His head light had gone out suddenly and was providing no more than a thready light. The scooter was heading towards bushes which the feeble light only enabled him to avoid just in time.

"Come on already!" the traveler exclaimed, in a fake cheerful tone.

The light was the only thing he had not checked before heading out. A broken light was just what he needed! He knew he couldn't count on finding any help. Once twilight came, there was no one to be found on those roads. All in all, he would have been better off taking the room he had been offered in Olmeto although 900 lira was a ridiculous price for a room like that, a room fit for a monsignor. Such a room would be hard to find in this neck of the woods in Calabria. And then there was also the waitress, a somewhat chubby brunette to be honest, but one who seemed willing enough, something that became obvious every time she came near him. If he expected the country girls in Santa Croce to make up for that...

Why had he been in such a rush to head out? There was no reason he absolutely had to reach the village the next day. Unless... he felt grotesque, his mood turned dark. Why did he have to suddenly justify his haste? And if he liked to drive at night, that was his choice, wasn't it? He dismissed his thoughts, but it was impossible for him to hide the fact for long that he wanted to stifle himself. And he knew that he was running away from himself, and only himself, into the night. Around him, dust swirled in the night and Mario drove forward as if toward deliverance.

The storm haunted every bit of the shadow where, silently, his fading headlight finally settled. The traveler felt uncomfortable. The uncertain light slid over the nocturnal felt like a clumsily thrown harpoon. He whistled a tune to cover the indiscrete purr of the Lambretta. Too bad if it was raining. The important thing was to get to his destination before the sole hotel closed.

Despite the movement, drops of sweat ran down Mario's face and back. A breath of hot air played abruptly over his face as he started down a partially visible slope.

Below, the road ran into the Scaricatori river where the deafening roar of steep waterfalls seemed to challenge the inanimate landscape. His headlight cast rusty bruises over the furious water. Mario was breathing better, but had to submit to the attack of transparent gnats blinded by the light. Moreover, the debris covered roadway grew narrower and narrower with each passing second, crossing the torrent on bridges without guardrails that twisted this way and that in sudden turns.

Hunched over his handlebar, eyes focused on the uneven ground, deafened by the roar of the water, he drove painfully slowly. And his throat grew tighter and tighter as he drove upward, drawing closer and closer to immense curtains of impenetrable, menacing darkness.

Silence cloaked the night as the Scaricatori river suddenly widened, as it continued to spew its foamy water. Mario heard a bell ring in the distance. While the tumult continued, the traveler, relieved by the thought of reaching his goal, accelerated. He sped onto a log bridge. His foot tensed on the brake. A black shape leapt out in front of him and when, as he lost his balance as a result of the surprise, and brushed against it, he heard violent, rapid panting. When he finally came to a stop, he turned around, but the apparition had vanished into the night.

Arms and legs trembling, Mario set out slowly. A violent wave of disgust sickened him. No, there was no doubt about it. The being he had trapped for a second in the beam of his headlight wore the old-fashioned clothing once worn by penitents during certain processions: a loose-fitting dark robe with a hood covering the wearer's face, with two holes for their eyes.

But what was that individual doing here, in the middle of the night and, above all, how had he managed to disappear so quickly?

"He did not walk down the road," thought Mario. "I turned around too quickly."

There was only one solution...

"No, no, that was impossible. He did not jump!"

A long day on the road, combined with the difficulty of the route, was making him vulnerable to fantasies born out of the night. Yet, a second later, he was uncertain about what he had seen.

The countryside suddenly burst into flame. A horrible cry rang out in the forced shadow, soared over the flickering light, then was quickly pummeled by the roll of thunder. In every corner of the sky, the storm converged on the Scaricatori river and the traveler, drowned by the blinding downpour, took shelter under the first rock he found.

He watched as the sky and the torrent engaged in a furious battle, pitting their water and noise against one another. The temperature cooled. Shivering, Mario kept his hand on the switchblade that never left his side. The monstrous cry continued to vibrate through him as he hunkered down in the dark against the wet rock, ready for anything.

The storm did not last. Although the sky did not clear, the rain stopped as suddenly as it had started. The drenched countryside rose out of its torpor. Mario set out on his way and, when the waters of the Scaricatori river calmed for a moment, he recognized the dismal hoot of fear.

Finally, he caught site of the white shape of the dam that looked down from the imposing slopes of Monte

Peccatore, where a late light continued to shine. At the side of the road, a tippy sign read: Santa Croce.

It seemed to him that the plain houses of the new village, slumbering around the dam, looked aggressive and bitter. Stifling his impressions, attributing them to fatigue, he looked for the hotel. It was slumbering as well and nothing set it aside from the other buildings apart from a large wooden sign nailed to the façade with half erased gold lettering that read: *Casa delle Viatore*.

Mario knocked at the door for a long time before noting any sign of life. Relief washed over him when he heard the sound of slippers dragging over cobblestones and half a face bloated with fat and sleep peered out from behind a partially opened door.

"Who's there?" asked a female voice, in almost a monotone.

"A room... I know it's late. But I had troubles with my headlight."

"And this damned weather doesn't make things any better," he added, to fill the silence that was growing heavy.

The woman watched Mario, undecided whether to open the door for him or not. She bent slightly forward and in the dim light the skin of her forehead looked dirty gray.

"I hope the hotel isn't closed" the traveler asked, suddenly concerned.

"Where are you coming from?" asked the woman in her surprisingly deep voice.

"Naples. So?"

"You've come here... why?"

"I'm a journalist. What's it to you? Do you want to rent me a room or not?"

131

He was starting to lose his patience. So much egoism or stupidity!

The woman continued to hesitate. She glanced at the Lambretta although she could only guess at the license plate rather than actually see it. Her distrust seemed to fade.

"Fine," she said, coldly. "But this is no time to be disturbing people."

Mario slipped his scooter under a lean-to attached to the side of the hotel. Picking up his suitcase, he followed the woman. Obviously, the dumpy matron was the innkeeper. Possibly, she might also be the maid and the cook. There might not be a large staff here. She climbed up the stairs heavily, her large body tilted to one side by the effort she made with her arm to pull herself up by the handrail. There were three rooms on the upper floor. As the only guest, Mario had his choice. Wanting above all to change his clothes and warm up, he walked into the first room and asked to have a grog brought up.

The woman looked at him with a bovine expression and turned away without a word.

He ran behind her, asking, "Can you bring me one?"

"Right away, right away," she replied softly.

And she headed off, feet dragging, hips rolling from side to side. Eyes drooping with fatigue, Mario watched her walk off.

He thought, "She's one of those people who no longer has any hope. She continues on her way. She does her job. Resigned."

He got undressed, rubbed himself energetically and pulled on his pajamas. In no time at all she was back. He took the steaming mug from her hands and smiled. She grimaced.

"Here," she said. "Fill out this form."

The sound of slippers dragging yet again. Mario gulped down the boiling grog and started to write. Family name: Salgari. First name: Mario. He yawned.

"That's it... I'll finish it tomorrow."

He took a deep breath and slid under the cool sheets.

CHAPTER II

In the velvety shadow of slumber, Mario saw a yellow plate, moving slowly, sometimes nearer, sometimes farther. He waved his arms in an effort to move it aside. In vain. He tried to turn away from it. In vain. The unsettling brightness continued to draw closer, covering him with its pasty, hot cast-iron weight. At the same time, as if to revive his numbed senses, slender needles dug into his flesh, spreading an irritating venom. By reflex, his arms spread in a tardy, childish gesture of defense, changing the position of his body. The yellow plate slipped sidewise to follow him.

He jumped up. The darkness seemed to vibrate around him and the astonishing vision froze against the opposite wall. Only then did Mario, his stomach heaving at the sight of the abrupt motionlessness, realize that he was looking through a window at a powerless, distant moon.

He ran toward the light, raised the metal trellis, with holes here and there in the latticework, that served as a screen and inhaled greedily. But no breath of air came from the petrified landscape. Suffocating, he looked up at the sky, which was as pale and heavy as the ceiling of a grotto poorly lit by an insufficient number of flashlights. Everything down here seemed to be waiting for the monstrous collapse of the blocks that formed the dam. The journalist tore his eyes away from the dam and allowed his gaze to roll over the deep gorges being carved by the Scaricatore river. Pale, syrupy gashes that looked, at this distance, like trails left by slugs.

"What am I doing here?" Mario muttered.

Obviously, this part of the country was just as he had been told: heavy, hostile. And an investigation would provide nothing more. Mario could just as well have written his report in his bedroom in Naples! He might just as well do nothing and head out on vacation as he had been preparing to do. No! He had wanted to come here. He had even insisted on it to his boss.

Moretti had looked at him like you look at an object that has been misplaced by the cleaning lady.

"Well, I thought you were on the Riviera?" he had said.

"That's for later. If you allow me to, I would like to postpone my vacation and take a trip to Santa Croce."

"I see."

The manager's eternal, ironic smile made it impossible to determine if he were truly surprised.

"As you wish," he finally said, sounding completely indifferent.

Mario shivered as he lowered the metal trellis. His hand encountered a mosquito drunk on blood and he brushed it against his chest like a crushed raspberry. He walked over to his suitcase and took out a tube of quinine pills, took two slim, blue tablets and walked over to the sink.

"Moretti has never taken me seriously," he thought. "This is what you want? Go ahead, old chap. Enjoy the trip! If I keep you on at the newspaper I do so only in memory of your father. You know that. fine! This time he'll get something for his money. I have no problem, no problem at all making up a story."

He lifted up the pitcher that was three-quarters empty and filled the large glass. Pills on his tongue, he took a large gulp. A horrible taste of decomposing plants filled his mouth and he immediately spat the repugnant liquid out. He held the pitcher up to the light. The water looked clear. How long had it been in the pitcher waiting for some hypothetical tourist? A taste of mold remained in Mario's mouth increasing the nausea he had felt since waking.

Hoping that moving about would do him some good, the young man dressed silently and slipped outside. It was the first time he had felt so unwell without having tied one on the previous night. No, this part of the country did not suit him. It was one thing, when finding himself in an unknown place, for his mind to be unsettled, that was perfectly natural, particularly if you have a penchant for mystery, if you enjoy frightening people. But for his body to be affected...

A fragile presence among the dark masses of the night, the small light continued to sparkle on the slope of Monte Peccatore. The darkness seemed filled with murderous desires and, as he walked aimlessly in the direction of the dam, which seemed to purr in the thick silence, he felt as if jealous eyes were following his footsteps. He slipped his left hand slowly into his pants pocket and his fingers closed over the rough handle of the knife. Then, just as slowly, he opened his fingers and withdrew his hand. Honestly, he was behaving like a child! Why was he conjuring up such terrors?

"Let's stick to the facts and try to remain objective," he said to himself.

He summed up what he knew and was unable to keep from frowning with scorn.

"What a story! On his way back from a trip, Moretti's brother-in-law had made a stop in Santa Croce. What did he find there? What everyone notices: an inhospitable setting. What did he learn? Objects disappear. What

136

kind of objects? Useless objects of no value: family portraits, post office calendars, tattered magazines, unused clothing. And where did he get this famous information from? From the people living there? No. From a jeering policeman from Mammola who could have even been bothered to go to the place in person. And as for me..."

He stopped. He thought he heard footsteps following him. No, nothing. A branch cracked. Mario kicked a clump of earth with the toe of his shoe. Perhaps he was disturbing someone or something? That thought was not at all displeasing to him.

He quickly reached the dam and stopped once again, placed his elbows on a guardrail and stood there, facing the reservoir. The blackish water was still. It looked miserably cold and, curiously enough, the mosquitoes had all vanished.

Mario remained there a long time, observing the liquid void. The mud that had been rising in the pit of his stomach gradually resided into a layer of silt. The pain faded and his mind, both empty and thoughtful, searched for the unfathomable. From time to time, the bell of the nearby church rang heavily. How many strokes? For how long? Night was fleeing without moving...

And never, ever, would he remember the first notes. If he heard the first notes... they were already in his memory when he shivered. A voice, a woman's voice, was whispering in his ear.

He looked around. The dam. chalky white walls of the dam did not give the shadow much room for retreat. He sighed to break the spell cast by this place and moved away. The sounds accompanied him and he had the impression they were coming to him through water. He bent down, almost lying down on the guardrail.

There was no doubt about it. The voice was rising up toward him and the screen of water that bound the notes and extended the end notes, modifying the naturally pure timber, added a delicate, quaint inflection to it.

Arms dangling, fingernails digging into his palms, Mario observed the dark, still water. And his heart started pounding violently when he realized—finally—that the singing voice was addressing him. His cheeks started to burn. Panting, he forced himself to adopt a more dignified posture. Once again, he exalted, once again, the rusty keys to a world that was possibly inaccessible tinkled before him. Erasing six months of a dreary, disenchanted life, the unknown voice painted him with joy touched by anguish. At the same time, childhood memories floated to the surface of his mind. He recognized the tune of the medieval lament, although the tones seemed somehow poorer, emptier to him. And... the words had been changed. Minimal alterations had given the lyrics a new and unsettled meaning. And as for the refrain that returned at the end of each couplet, Mario did not recall having heard it anywhere and the meaning seemed cryptic to him as occasionally happens in old romances.

When the voice fell silent, allowing the leaden mantle of the night to fall back over his shoulders, the unusual refrain echoed in his mind for a long time:

What is the life between us worth
If death loves you?

The whiteness of the dam seemed unbearable to him and, far too troubled to even consider sleeping, he crept away like a thief from the tangled slopes of Monte Peccatore.

CHAPTER III

He pinched his cigarette out between his fingers. A little below him, in the dense glade, a human shape was moving stealthily. With each step, it would stop, listen, then set out again furtively. A branch, no doubt dead, broke in its hands. The figure grabbed onto the closest tree trunk and clung there. The hideous panting Mario had noticed a few hours earlier returned as Mario searched through the night, finding two feverish eyes. Then the forge bellows quieted and, after a terribly long moment, the enigmatic creature continued on its way. The journalist was standing there, still, when a spot of light revealed the creature to him. Nausea suddenly swept over him.

Could it be possible! The woman's body was completely covered in tattered rags, making her look like a walking scarecrow. The blouse, which was far too large, hung in tatters over the remnants of a pleated skirt, riddled with holes, that failed to hide mud-covered legs. A grotesque straw hat, frayed along one side and decorated with artificial fruits, crowned the head of the apparition, which had already vanished back into the night.

Mario bent down to light his cigarette and puffed on it deeply, hand curved in front of the red light to hide it. The bell rang three o'clock. He hesitated. Should he go back? He could care less about his investigation! Only one thing concerned him at this point: the sordid creature was ruining the space of the waking dream into which the charming voice of the lake had transported him. Her damned panting hid the fluid song he would never grow

139

tired of hearing. And now it was over. Now the tone had lost its purity and dark anxiety pinched Mario's heart.

He was already starting to have doubts. He knew that no human being could get that close to water intakes without running the risk of getting caught up in the current, which would pitch the body against the steel grates, where it would be flattened, then shredded into a messy pulp in just a few seconds. Moreover, how could the voice have come from under the water? He must have imagined it. But why would he have done that, if not out of some need to use a liberating hallucination to set aside the disappointing, hopeless setting?

But reality got the upper hand. All he had to do was follow the repugnant creature, catch the thief—since it could only be her, of course— in the act and have her arrested. That's why he had come to Santa Croce. To drag the homeless pack of rags off to prison. How petty! He'd be better off heading back to the hotel right away. Yes, he'd head back, walking past the dam, walking slowly, ever so slowly, past the dam.

Pebbles rolled under his feet. With a few strides, he found himself back at the shore of the lake, covered with juniper and myrtle, releasing violent scents. And soon he found himself back at the edge of the wood from which he could see the clear line of the dam. Poor shacks hunkered next to it in the shadow, sleeping.

Cries tore through the night. One silhouette appeared, one that was all too easy to recognize, followed by a second, white and slender.

An outburst hid a child's laments, "Jesus bambino! What a shame!"

Panting again. The disgusting creature was running straight toward Mario. She finally noticed him and stopped short, moaning like an injured beast. Then she turned back, narrowly avoiding being struck by the candelabra the shrieking shape was brandishing over her head.

"Satan's servant!" the shape shouted, awkwardly making the sign of the cross with her left hand, while swinging the heavy candelabra in circles around her thin body.

Then she too noticed Mario and immediately retreated in the direction of the house where a child wailed. After attempting to make her way through the juniper trees, which were impassible at that point, the miserable creature in rags wandered over to the dam where the intense light swallowed her up. There she curled up into a quivering ball in the deepest section of shadow.

Mario continued to walk ahead. He felt that the two women were stiff with fear. Suddenly, the pack of rags stood up and rushed along the path of the light, convulsively waving her ghostly, fleshless arms scattering shreds of her clothing over the bushes.

"Where did she come from?" the journalist asked the second woman, who was standing in front of the door clasping the candelabra to her chest with both hands.

The woman looked him up and down. She had small, bright eyes, hardened by the almost total absence of eyelashes. The white bonnet that hid her hair and a large portion of her forehead and the shapeless nightgown she wore made it impossible for him to determine her age.

"I don't know you," she said, turning cautiously to go inside.

Mario shrugged carelessly.

"I'm not a werewolf."

"There's no need to be walking about at this time of night."

She reached for the bolt, which creaked.

"I'm not the only one," said Mario... "I'm not the only one walking about."

"May she go to hell!"

The woman spat on the ground.

"And what about me?" asked Mario.

She looked at him, bewildered.

"Can I go to hell as well?"

"I don't know you. Good evening."

"Good evening."

Mario took a few steps. The woman did not move.

"Fine, she wants to talk..." thought Mario.

He turned back, smiled and said, "I'm from Naples..."

Silence.

"...and I plan to go back there as soon as possible."

He motioned in the direction of the dam and asked, "Is she the thief?"

The woman flinched at those words.

"I don't know her," she shouted, brandishing the candelabra. "No, I don't know her. I've never seen her before. May she never come back."

Her jaw clenched and the words she was spitting out grew unintelligible. Mario saw a tear slide down the bridge of her nose.

"Lo bambino..."

The journalist paid close attention. In vain. Suddenly, the memory of what she had seen roused the peasant. Her narrow chest swelled. Her anger burst and she shouted, "My son, that shameful woman was holding him in her arms. She was rocking him, hugging him.

Carogna! Did she kiss him? I saw her from behind. The bitch! I was sleeping too soundly!"

She flailed her arms and continued, saying "She heard me stir. She put him down and ran off. I should have... I should have.... Perhaps she did kiss him... My God! What should I do?"

Overwhelmed, she started to sob. The child's cries gradually calmed, then doubled in intensity. With a serious expression on his face, Mario had walked over to the woman. He placed his hand gently on her shoulder. She stiffened and leapt away. She fled, slamming the door in his face. Behind it, she chortled.

"Ah! Ah! They know my man is dead and no one lives in these shacks. They know I'm all alone in this place. I'll defend myself! By the holy Virgin, I'll defend myself..."

"Defend yourself against who?" Mario shouted, dumbfounded.

"Anything! I know what I'm saying. And what's it to you? you're going back to Naples, aren't you? Don't pay any attention to anyone and go back to bed. It's not good to be walking about at this time of night."

"I'm sorry," said the young man. "I would have liked to help you."

"Help me? You know me well enough to help me? I'm nothing to you! Help me! Ha! What you want is to know things. An unhealthy curiosity. That's all! Well, if it's so important to you, go ask old Benedetto why he leaves his light on all night..."

"Who is Benedetto?"

Mario received no response. He asked other questions, Without any success. The woman had decided not to utter another word. He returned to the dam and melancholically considered the now silent water. His thoughts were in turmoil. The reasonable part of his mind tried to view the disturbing events of the recent hours as aberrations caused by fatigue and the change in scenery. But the peasant's ambiguous words and her fear indicated that the phenomenon was at the least unusual. And the panting of the woman in rags connected her in a sinister manner to another apparition. It was becoming impossible for him to deny one without denying the other. And if Mario accepted both of them, if he could prove to himself that, in both cases, he was not the victim of hallucinations, how could he continue to reject the reality of the lake's enigmatic voice. Yet, he reared up warily at that thought, knowing just how fascinating he found the irrational.

An enormous racket blurred his thoughts. The gates of the dam opened, releasing tons of foaming water downstream. On the verge of going back to his room, Mario glanced around one last time. Above, like a buoy tied to the drifting night, a vigilant light continued to shine.

CHAPTER IV

The path was vanishing second by second into the bush and Mario was growing tired looking for it. In the distance, the storm rumbled weakly... or perhaps that sound was just the water in the lake crashing in the depths of the gorges? At this distance distinguishing between the two was difficult. A sort of gangrene was sweeping over the sky where the moonbeams still cast light here and there, then grew dark before touching the peaks of the trees. The reservoir was no longer visible, but its presence was more tangible, more significant as the journalist walked up. Some dangers only become apparent when you move farther away from them. Also, people generally prefer to adventure into the unknown than to turn back.

His face and arms covered with scratches, Mario walked on like a robot. He never took his eyes from the small light, even when the soles of his shoes slipped on the grass. He knew that he should avoid thinking, that above all he should avoid asking questions before he reached the farm. He listened, he looked, he walked. Somewhere, a toad started croaking.

His feet in water, Mario had to stop yet again. An almost silent creek was blocking the path, which seemed once again to come to an end. Thinking that he was now close to his goal, the journalist wasted no time on pointless searching and slipped between the bushes. But, since he was constantly forced to dip beneath the leaves of tangled branches, he feared he would lose sight of the light and, once he escaped from their embrace, his lost eyes searched avidly through the night.

A flash of lightning cast a metallic light over the landscape covered with barbed-wire fences where black pines stood like miradors. Instead of exploding, the thunder rolled in a long lament and Mario shivered, afraid to clearly examine the vision of himself he had just received: a vision of a prisoner vainly seeking escape, a prisoner lost in the immense defense mechanisms of an abandoned camp incapable of attracting the attention of his jailors. Adding to his displeasure, he felt fragile bones crack and his foot sunk into something soft. He stepped back, uttering a muffled cry. He had crushed the body of a partially decomposed crow.

"Imbecile!" he exclaimed, furious. "What did you think it was? A vampire?"

But in the brief moment he had bent down to look at the beast, the light had disappeared.

He kicked the carcass furiously out of the way. Then, thinking his shoe must be covered with filth, he wiped it vigorously on the grass. His passion waned and, with a wicked joy, he now gave free rein to all of the doubts he had managed to contain.

"Well, aren't you making great progress! Moreover, what did you expect? That the old man would welcome you with open arms like the prodigal son? That's not really how people behave around here... Definitely not! You were just walking around and you saw the light, so... In passing, you take an interest... you're polite. The old man is pleased to have a visitor. You chat a bit. Since he knows the rules of hospitality, he invites you into his home for a drink. And completely naturally you ask Signor Benedetto why he leaves the light on all night."

"The bastard," grumbled Mario. "He should have turned it off!"

Large drops of rain crashed, hissing, into the thickets and raced down into his shirt. In a few minutes his teeth would be chattering. Meanwhile, he felt tired and discouraged as if he had spent a night drinking and hollering. And yet, just a little earlier, in the heat of excitement, he had set out!

"It's terrible," he thought. "It's terrible, just how drunk you can get on a single idea. I set out without thinking, without taking time to consider just how absurd my plans were. Why did I need to go check the fields for that old peasant's rags! And, all in all, if Benedetto uses up his electricity out of some fear of God or for some other reason, one had to be fairly presumptuous to hope to interview him in the middle of the night. It would be better to head back to the hotel right away."

Yet, some unconscious concern or perhaps a vague foreboding of danger distracted him and he found good reasons for continuing his adventure. Would it not be ridiculous to give up when he was so close to his goal and the storm would prevent him from returning to the hotel? Moreover, if he did find the farm, he could always ask for shelter, which would give him an opportunity to initiate the conversation...

He headed for the side where the light had first appeared. But he quickly lost his way and realized this when he recognized a partially uprooted holm oak he had tripped over earlier. Fortunately, a flash of lightning revealed a nearby clearing and the wall of a building with a bull's eye window just under the roof.

He fumbled about as he walked, then found a wet fence. He immediately took a step back. The metal trellis shook violently, then bent at shoulder height as warm breath struck his face. Howling and the sound of chains dragging reassured him. Other dogs joined in and their racket filled the darkness. Mario congratulated himself. The alarm had been sounded. There would be no need for him to wade about in the mud, waiting for the old man to wake.

He walked along the fence, making sure not to touch it. Soon, a weak light tinted the bare soil of the yard red and the trellis was replaced by a wooden gate which quickly turned to the left. He found himself standing in front of the farmhouse, which was partially hidden by a giant fig tree. Two lights shone, vanishing into the thick branches of the tree, their gleam drawing the thin stream of water forming at his feet from the shadow.

The dogs barked relentlessly. The most furious was the one who had sounded the alarm. He was chained behind the building. His shrieks egged the pack on. Mario wiped his forehead, his eyes. He slicked his dripping hair back. One of the lit rooms caught his attention since he had just seen the shape of a man walk through it. The light bulb, not protected by any lampshade, hung in the middle of the room, casting a brutal light over the once white walls now covered by soot thrown there produced by smoking meat over a fire made with green wood. The beams were blackened as well and too low. The floor was made of beaten dirt. No furniture? Yes. Mario could make out a massive table in one corner, probably accompanied by one or two benches.

The silhouette reappeared in the window frame and stood there motionless. It was an old man. He was holding a gun, inspecting it. And his extraordinarily wrinkled face seemed to be laughing.

"He's crazy!" thought Mario.

That idea, both tenacious and sudden, paralyzed him. Another idea, no less unsettling, followed the first: had the woman sent him to the old man just to get rid of him? Did she not realize the risk she was making him take? He closed his eyes and forced himself to stop thinking for a few moments. Then he would be able to consider things calmly. Indubitably, Santa Croce was awash in an atmosphere of unease, if not actually anguish, which could not be attributed to small thefts committed by prowlers. As for the rest, why had that beggar woman approached a sleeping child? No matter what the situation was, frightened people were dangerous. It would be a good idea for him to keep his mind clear and avoid creating terrors from random impressions. If the old man let him get close...

"Yes, but for now, I could well get shot," he thought.

The window cracked open. The man poked his head out, paying no attention to the rain, and shouted, "You're less afraid of the light than the lightning! Come one now, show yourself!"

Mario slipped deeper into the shadow.

"You're not afraid of the dogs. I know that. Why would you be afraid of the dogs, wretch?"

A flash of lightning lit up the whitewashed walls.

"Why?" repeated the old man. "Why? Why?"

The howls of the dogs hid his powerful voice.

"Quiet!" he shouted. "Lupo, Drago, Furia, be quiet. Sciabola, Rossicio, lie down!"

The dogs dragged their chains, whimpering.

"They obey well, don't they?" the old man said with a satisfied smile. "You're not afraid of them, I know... But they warn me. That's all I ask them to do. Now, let's get over with it. You came because the light was burned out. Only you didn't plan on the storm... Come on, show yourself and talk if you want to."

"Completely crazy!" thought Mario, returning to his initial idea despite himself.

He searched for his knife with icy fingers.

"Mary Mother of God, if you don't step out of your hole, I'll come down and pull you out..."

A pale shape crossed through the room. A young girl, a very young girl, frail and shivering.

"No, no, please... Don't go out," she begged, throwing herself into the old man's arms.

"Angelina, go back to bed," grumbled the old man.

"I'm afraid..."

She crossed herself and said, "Close the window, Papa. Don't go out. Your gun is no good against them. We have to pray..."

He pushed her aside gently.

"Leave me be, little one. I want to know what they want. And since I've got one here, by Christ, he'll tell me."

He turned to look out the window, shook his fist and shouted "We're not afraid. But we are tired of hearing you prowling about!"

Angelina burst into tears. She wept almost silently, standing straight, frozen, in the middle of the room. Her shining eyes, her bright red lips, stood out against her chalky white, hollow face. Mario, who was watching her closely, found the anxious, resigned expression on her face unsettling. The word *victim* came to his mind.

The old man caressed his daughter's hair. His deeply tanned face was riddled with wrinkles that pulled all of his features upward, lifting the corners of his mouth, his nostrils, the outer edges of his eyelids and his eyebrows. His face was both kind and crafty, indolent and obstinate, like the faces on Etruscan sculptures. His gesture revealed tenderness and distress. Mario felt sympathy for the unknown old man and the child.

"Signor Benedetto," he called out in a calm voice.

He had just, a little late it must be admitted, made a connection between the old man's invective and the terror expressed by the strange person he had surprised in the Lambretta's light. Certainly, the old man must have encountered that individual, several times perhaps, and not all on his own, as indicated by his words. And he had drawn his own conclusions. No, the man was not crazy.

Hearing his name called out, the old man jumped. And the dogs went back to barking. He had to shut them up again.

"Signor Benedetto, I'm not afraid of the storm or your lights, but please tie up your dogs..."

"What's all this?" grumbled the old man. "It seems like this is no time to be hanging around outside... The tarantulas will be biting, boy."

"Perhaps... But why do you keep your light on if you don't want to attract the bugs that are prowling about like me... or like those you fear?"

The old man's cheeks flamed. He brandished his gun in the direction of the fig tree.

"Come out of there! You hear me? Come out of there or I'll shoot you! I do what I want here. I'm the master here, in God's name, and I fear what I want to fear."

Angelina murmured something the journalist could not hear.

"That's fine," said Benedetto. "Show yourself."

"Tie up your dogs, first," repeated Mario.

The old man shrugged. Mario saw him disappear, with the young girl on his heels. Two seconds later, the door creaked and he stepped out. Angelina stayed behind, trembling, on the threshold, unknowingly undressed by the light shining behind her.

Did the man's gait seem uncertain, hesitant, because he had to pick his way around the puddles formed by the downpour? No, he really was limping and when he got a little closer Marios caught a glimpse of the brown, round shape of a wooden leg peeking out under the corduroy pants. The ongoing clanking of shapes converged in the direction of the farmer and two mastiffs joined him in front of the gate. He caressed them with his hands and his knee.

"Where are you?"

"Here…"

The beam of a flashlight blinded Mario and questions rang out.

"Who are you? Where are you from?"

He replied honestly and tried to explain with just a few words, but there was no accounting for his behavior. He was unable to completely relieve Benedetto's mistrust. The old man was furious at being caught off guard by a stranger, forced into discussing uncommon matters.

And when Mario, in turn, dared to ask a question, the old man replied brutally, "I don't like interrogations, boy, and I have nothing to say. What I think is my business."

He inhaled noisily, then said, "You and your kind make a muddle of everything. I don't plan to end my days in an asylum."

"As you wish, Signor, I... I have no intention of..."

"Enough," interrupted the old man. "You wanted to get me drenched by the storm. Well, you've done just that. Now, be on your way."

Mario caught the old man by the lapel of his coat, running the risk of being attacked by one of the dogs.

"Listen, I'm drenched too, and cold... can I come in for a moment to warm up? It will be morning soon."

The old man looked at him with narrowed eyes. His eyelids were covered with wrinkles.

"Wait a second," he said. "I'll tie up the dogs. Then you can come in."

Mario raced across the courtyard. He had to bend down to go through the door. Angelina, hands once again protecting her chest, stared at him.

CHAPTER V

They had pulled the bench in front of the fireplace where the coals were already turning black and, sitting side by side, they each pursued the same line of thought. Outside, the storm had calmed. All they could hear now was the clanking of chains on the rough soil of the courtyard and, when a breath of wind shook the fig tree, the crashing of large raindrops in the puddles.

Mario was swirling an old maraschino liqueur the old man had served him in a silver cup. A connoisseur, he appreciated the perfumed warmth. He never took his half-closed eyes away from the sparkling fireplace where extravagant constructions took shape then fell into ruin. It seemed that time had stopped or that it had benevolently decided to stand still. In the next room, Angelina was sleeping like a baby.

The old man got up to make some mush for the dogs. While cutting thick slices of black bread over a pot half filled with sour milk, he never took his eyes off Mario and his lips trembled as if, on the verge of saying something, he suddenly held back. Yet, the journalist had confided in him. He had told him about the reasons for his investigation, about the phenomena he had witnessed. While listening to him, Benedetto had nodded his head, without commenting. Finally, almost against his will, he decided to talk.

"You see..." he said in a solemn tone. "You see, they never should have done that."

Surprised, Mario turned to look at him. Eyes lowered, the old man seemed to be thinking. Perhaps he was feeling intimidated? Perhaps Mario should have been more formal?

"There were plenty of waterfalls where they could have built that dam. Instead, they flooded the village. That's not good... not good at all."

"You liked the old village?" Mario asked.

"Oh, personally... I've always had my farm here. Only, it's not the same... dour old ones are down there, the ones who built Santa Croce, where it used to be. The old ones... All our old ones... we've done them wrong. Of course, they haven't complained, and for good cause, but they weren't pleased. You can believe me. When they moved the cemetery, it was not a pretty sight. Gravediggers came from Olmeto, breaking this, tearing that apart... The dug up everything... It was worse than a bombing..."

"The dead could not just be abandoned," Mario said, gently.

The old man grew angry.

"It would have been better to leave them where they were. You don't understand. What are those dead people doing in the new cemetery? Does the new village concern them? They're like strangers... It's as if the graves had been robbed. And the village, the village hunkered down there with not a single dead person left? When do you ever see a dead village without a single dead person? And God as well... They tore down his house. Even if he wanted to return to his chapel he can't. The stained-glass windows, the bells, everything was removed. And the floor tiles in the church were broken because the priests' bones were buried under them. They made it worse than a barn! That was ten years ago. I told them. That wasn't good, not good at all... that just amused them. So, what happened, well it happened and we see things that are not ordinary."

Benedetto fell silent, no doubt hoping for some word of encouragement, but the journalist remained silent. That sententious meandering had irritated and disappointed him. The old man closed his knife, picked up a jar of tobacco from the fireplace mantle, and rolled a cigarette. The wrinkles on his face grew deeper, highlighting his concern.

"Your maraschino liqueur is truly marvelous," Mario said, hoping to relax the atmosphere.

He felt that his tone sounded fake.

The old man smiled briefly, but warmly.

"I made it before the dam was built. Angelina had just started walking and her mother was still alive. He took a few steps, eyes riveted on the floor.

"One day, we wanted to see Reggio and the sea. We never went out. Why that day? We took the bus at Olmeto. Just before we reached Reggio it drove into a ravine. My wife was killed instantly. As for me…"

He slapped his wooden leg with his hand.

"I'm not used to speaking so much," he murmured. "I keep to myself. But what you did this evening is not usual and I told myself that possibly you would understand certain things."

"You took your time!" thought Mario.

"You see, it's not easy to explain," continued the old man. "I know what you were thinking just then. The crazy old man believes in ghosts. That's it, eh? Ghosts? I'd like that."

He crossed himself quickly.

"It's worse."

He poured himself half a glass of maraschino liqueur and handed the bottle to the young man.

"It started last year, just at the end of the summer. I was preparing to kill the pig and I had gone down next to the reservoir to a place where the aromatic plants I needed grow. It was very hot and I was rushing. Night fell and I had not finished picking. At that time of day, you know, the cicada suddenly stopped singing. Then, in the silence, I heard a sound like a deep sigh, then another, then another. I was quite surprised since there was no wind. Furia who had followed me started growling... She was looking at the lake and did not want me to approach it. I don't much like things I can't explain... I was listening to that as I was picking my herbs and I wasn't terribly pleased."

He nodded his head and swirled the maraschino in his glass.

"The dog was pacing around me. The fur on her back was standing up and she had bared her fangs. She caught the scent of something disgusting. She noticed it before I did... But I did notice it too. I don't think I've ever smelled anything worse. The terrible odor came from the water. Unbearable! We had to get out of there. And that evening, I didn't mention it to anyone. Not even my girl, but..."

He threw his cigarette nervously into the fireplace and nodded, saying, "That was the first time! The next day and the next after that I returned to the lake with the dogs. Nothing. If Furia had not been with me when it happened, I would have wound up believing I had dreamed. Then winter came, a hard winter. Do you remember? It snowed here for several days. Sometimes I would set snares. All that section of the forest that runs 500 meters from the farm to the reservoir belongs to me. I do what I want there! One morning, as I was walking down there—I had taken a cane since it's easy to stumble there—I get to the lake and what do I see? The snow was packed down, flattened, as if someone had dragged a body at least the size of a sheep there. It started from a point where the shore is low and clear and headed into the wood. I followed that most unusual trail. Suddenly, it stopped short. And just there, at that spot, I saw one of my snares with a large hare trapped in it. It was obvious that someone had moved my snare. I bent down, suspicious, to look at the animal. In the snow, next to the body, I saw tufts of fur that had been torn out. I thought that someone had been there before me. With the tip of my stick, I turned the hare over. It had been gutted! The innards had been gnawed at, cleaned... Who could possibly have done that? A weasel would have bled it. But it did not look as if it had been bled. There was frozen blood all around the body. A fox? A fox would have carried it off. I decided to take a closer look. Honestly, it would have better for me to head straight home and try to forget everything. And do you know what I found when I examined it?"

Mario shrugged.

"Teeth marks. There was no mistaking it. whatever had gnawed at the animal had to be either a man or a woman. And when I stood back up and looked back at the frozen trail that led back to the lake, well... It wasn't hot that day but sweat was pouring down my forehead. The thoughts running through my mind were so stupid I didn't dare mention anything in the village. I simply told my girl not to go near the lake since I'd seen wolf tracks there and I would be setting traps."

The old man looked at Mario, then continued, saying "I spent the entire day doing that. The next day, I found one of the traps torn up. The steel teeth were covered with a thick rust. And, like the day before, the crushed snow formed a trail from the trap to the lake. This time I was certain! I stood guard for three days. Naturally, nothing unusual happened and I caught a bad cold that kept me at home until the thaw. One fine day, I felt better and got up. Down at the lake, two more traps had been uprooted. It was impossible to follow the trail but here and there the soil was all torn up and low branches had been torn off and lay in the mud. The same day—it was almost noon and I'll never forget it—in a small pond still covered with ice, I saw with my very own eyes a handprint. A woman's handprint, of course... And there was a finger missing..."

He placed his glass on the table.

"So, I finally mentioned all this to someone, then someone else, just to find out if I was the only one who had noticed anything... No one had seen anything. And I paid for my openness. Yet that all changed in the spring when things started disappearing. Oh, not anything valuable: a broken umbrella, torn shoelaces, a pot that was no longer being used, calendars and, above all, almanacs. People didn't care about what was taken, but they didn't like the fact that someone was going into their homes to take them. Particularly since they didn't know how it was being done. I do believe that some complaints were filed. Imagine that! Like the police would come here for a few missing trinkets. Meanwhile, people in Santa Croce grew distrustful and, since I was the first one to see unnatural things, they almost accused me of witchcraft. Now, whenever I go into the village there's always someone that insults me. Angelina is spared that. They seem to feel sorry for her because she has to live with me. You can rest assured that if I could send her somewhere else, I would have done that a long time ago. But I need her for the farm. And, as for selling this piece of land and going somewhere else, well, I've lived here too long. Anyway... It's my business and I'm boring you."

"Not at all," said Mario, listening closely.

Benedetto continued, "When the weather is good, my daughter goes up the mountain to watch over our goats. Sometimes, she sleeps in a small shack I built for her when I was younger. She takes supplies with her for two, three days, sometimes a week. This year, I was unhappy to see her set out all alone, but I let her go anyway. When she came back down, her eyes were wide and her knees were knocking. Angelina's not too fearful, for a girl. It had to be something serious. Well, someone had strangled her dogs while she was sleeping and one goat had disappeared. I found it that evening near the lake. But someone had milked it and her udder was covered with stinky, black pustules. She was bleating plaintively and seemed to be suffering a great deal. I killed her and burned the body."

Mario shifted his position. He was hesitant to believe this extravagant tale.

Yet Benedetto continued. "It was around the same time that the dogs started refusing to go near the lake. And I don't think I was the only one who heard the laments and groans. Everyone in the village was wondering what it all meant. But no one, not a single person, spoke to the authorities in the city. Because people in the city would have made fun of them. Take, for example, the doctor who has been on leave here for four or five months. Ask him what he thinks of things. He's seen nothing, heard nothing. And if you insist, he'll find some simple explanation. Good grief! All these thunderstorms at the lake... That's not normal... But I tell you *they* are

160

calling. *They* attract the lightning and *they* know it. *They're* afraid."

Mario was unable to hide a skeptical expression.

"The time of the storms," he said evasively.

Benedetto shook his head, without noting the remark.

"Perhaps that's why they're afraid of anything that shines, of anything that makes flames" the old man declared. "Look, I saw one myself, a few days ago. The one wearing the monk's robe, like you said and he was panting like beast. When I pointed my flashlight at his hood, he screamed. He vanished in a flash and I heard the terrible sound of a body falling into the water."

The farmer nodded his head as he looked at Mario, then said, "You're not following me anymore. I know you aren't! You don't like thinking about this aspect of the matter and the fact that they can come from the lake…"

"That's true," acknowledged Mario. "The facts are disturbing. I'm not questioning your good faith… But to go from there to concluding…"

"Conclude… conclude… conclude," interrupted the old man bitterly. "You have to come to some sort of conclusion. I'm telling you what I've seen and heard, that's all. And what about your monk that suddenly disappeared? Do you even wonder where he went? Conclusions! What's the point? If only we could destroy them. That would be fine with me."

He grinned knowingly and hurried to say, "But you won't walk away, not yet. I prefer to wait. Spend two or three evenings walking around the lake and then we'll talk about it again. You'll have to decide quickly since they're growing bolder and bolder… It hasn't been a long time since we've been seeing them, well before they started coming out... that proves they're taking fewer and fewer precautions. I also think they had to get used to their outings and when I think about the packed snow, I wonder what they looked like at the beginning..."

Mario was growing increasingly worried, despite his skepticism.

"Now, as soon as night falls, they're moving about," said Benedetto. "My girl went down to the village yesterday and said people had seen them this week. People will make complaints, of course, but for the police to come here..."

He shrugged.

"But that's not all. Up to now, those in the lake always wear robes and hoods while your beggar, well I know where her rags come from. I have a small garden down below where I grow a few vegetables... Well, I use rags to make scarecrows. So, if they start dressing like us, how will we recognize them?"

Suddenly overwhelmed, Benedetto fell silent as he fiddled nervously with the now empty cup. Silence shook both men like a wave.

"Wait," the old man said quickly. "I want to show you something I found in the courtyard the day before yesterday."

He headed over to a low door that opened onto a ruin and came back immediately, bent over by the weight of a completely rusted object which he placed on the floor near the fireplace.

"Do you know what this is?" fit-il d'un air entendu.

"Good grief! Iron boots, like those used in the Middle Ages. Do they come from the lake as well?" Mario replied.

The old man nodded.

"It's clear to me. I'm in danger. I've shown too much interest in their business, you know?"

The light went out and they realized day had come.

"Ah! It's you, sweetheart," the old man said without turning around. "You startled us..."

Angelina came over to embrace her father and gave her hand timidly to Mario. Then she set out to prepare breakfast. She worked in silence, glancing at the journalist from time to time. As the coffee was heating on the stove, she placed bowls and thick slices of bread in front of the two men, who were staring at the motionless trees outside without really seeing them.

"One more night!" sighed the old man.

After drinking his coffee, he wiped his lips on his sleeve.

"Now, I'm going to sleep a bit. They don't dare come around during the day."

Mario shook a knotty hand.

"Come back to see me some time," said Benedetto "I'll show you the places where I've seen things. If we could... I believe that time is of the essence."

He walked off slowly, a thin silhouette, back stooped under an invisible burden. The young man understood that Benedetto's generosity was restrained out of fear. The old man did not want to drag Mario into some monstrous adventure despite himself. "Come back to see me sometime" he'd said. Then he'd added "Time is of the essence" as he looked at Angelina.

Mario stood up in turn and bid farewell to the young girl. As he was walking through the door, she ran after him and placed something in his hand.

"Here," she murmured. "Keep it carefully."

Cheeks burning, she raced off. Mario looked at the small object she had given him. It was a blue enamel medal, with a picture of the Virgin. Touched, he walked off through the dense landscape. The morning was already warm. His mind felt empty as it often does following a great expenditure of nervous energy. The picture of those two living beings he'd just spent time with filled his mind, chasing away the fantasies of the previous evening. Yet, Benedetto's tale followed him, bringing them back to life, conferring on them a disastrous reality in which the mysterious voice of the lake insinuated itself like a troubled oasis in a merciless desert. Everything fit and, just like the bark of the trees along his path his hand might well, this very night or later, encounter rough homespun fabric.

The inert, gray day seemed to be lying, sickening and disgusting him.

CHAPTER VI

This time, Mario did not have to make much of an effort to find his way. The slope of the terrain helped him, as did the daylight, which had returned, a pale, foggy daylight like those strange haloes that announce a warm, rainy day.

Mario thought about the storm. Since arriving in Santa Croce, he'd had the impression that he was prowling around a lightning rod. The village and its surroundings seemed to be bathed in electricity. It poured down from the top of Monte Peccatore, drowning the houses, flowing over the dam, moving on regretfully, giving the water of the Scaricatore river its pale hue. Liquid lightning... A slow current that caused nerves to vibrate and made the senses unpleasantly, almost painfully sharp. The heart got involved, beating in counterpoint, adding to the general discord.

Mario avoided the shrubs with their dagger-like thorns. As he made his way through them, he tried to clarify the meaning of Benedetto's meanderings. Whatever it was they hid, they did fit, in some catastrophic manner, with the strangeness of this chaotic landscape and the motionless tension of the air, as taut as the string of a crossbow. They also fit in with the two grotesque, unsettling apparitions Mario had witnessed. Not to mention the liquid voice...

The lake was nearby. The journalist had reached a spot fairly far from the dam, between two promontories separated by a small cove. Marios headed in the direction of the pebbly beach.

Eyes heavy with sleep, he stared at the opposite shore, half hidden by the gray steam that rose from the water, which was as motionless as a molten lead plate. He was asleep on his feet. If he intended to pursue his investigation—and what an investigation it was—at this pace he wouldn't last 48 hours... He looked for a protected place where he could rest for an hour and lay down on the thick greenery. The ground was hard, but he could have slept on a fairground... He fell deeply asleep in a few seconds, his mind bustling with incomplete ideas and monstrous shapes.

Something woke him abruptly. He stood up, frightened, and looked around. It took him several seconds to reconnect with his memories of the previous night and realize what he was doing there.

He had no doubt slept less than an hour since the fog had not yet vanished from the surface of the lake. Tattered clouds rolled in a smokey sky low over the hills where the sun hung as a blinding yet blurry stain.

He stretched, thinking "Sometimes an hour of sleep is more restful than an entire night."

His eyes grew round. Beyond the reeds, he saw the shape of a boat drifting slowly between the two promontories. A woman sitting comfortably in the boat was staring at him.

He stood up. With a movement that seemed ghostly through the fog on the lake, the woman grasped the oars hooked to the gunwale and started rowing slowly in the direction of the shore. She must have been rowing earlier, and no doubt it was the noise of the oars hitting the water that had roused Mario from his sleep.

Convinced that there was some secret connection with the events of the previous evening, Mario walked closer to the water. A light breeze rippled the surface in the opposite direction of the waves created by the boat and a thousand small, fluffy suns quivered there in a mosaic. The boat scraped the stones on the bottom of the lake.

"Are you coming?" the woman asked.

Barely out of her teens, she was not truly a woman. The lines of her face were pure and her eyes were large and very dark. Her hair was black as well and flowed in curls to her shoulders, reminding Mario of the Florentine portraits of the Quattrocento. She wore a pale blue dress with a gold trimmed neckline.

Despite the unusual character of such a proposal, Mario did not hesitate to step into the water with his shoes on and climb into the boat. It's not every day a Madonna invites you for a trip on a lake... Mario smiled inside. There was something conventional about this new adventure. But such conventions apply to fairy tales, not reality, even including the dress the young girl wore, which Ariosto would have referred to as a "dress the color of morning."[2] Nothing in all this fit in with an investigation into petty larceny committed by beggars...

Once he was on board, everything went sour. Mario had grasped the oars and the fog enveloped them more quickly than it should have. From the shore, it had only looked thick in the middle of the lake.

"You are..." Mario started to say as he pulled of the oars.

He had been about to say "as nice as you are beautiful" and stopped himself just in time. The young girl was obviously not from around here. She was a city girl...

---

[2] This probably refers to Ariosto's *Orlando Furioso* (Note from the Translator)

accustomed to well-worded compliments. He did not intend to bore her with platitudes.

But she prevented him from looking any longer.

"Francesca..." she said, in a veiled, distant voice.

Mario took a second to realize that she had completed the sentence he had started in her own manner.

"Francesca da Ricci..." she added.

She continued, as if speaking to herself.

"Old family… very old line…" With that last word, she gave him a small, mysterious smile.

Mario shrugged, breaking the spell.

"It's very kind of you to have invited me to climb on board your boat…" he said, sounding just as stupid as he had earlier.

He was annoyed with himself. Usually at ease talking with girls in Napoli, he felt mired down in the fog, by the heavy, frozen climate of this backwoods.

"My name… My name is Mario Salgari..." he added.

He looked at Francesca's eyes, as she continued to stare at him.

"You're not from around here?" he asked.

"My family…" she started to say.

She fell silent, looked away and dipped her slender fingers into the water. Mario did not insist. Something weighed down his tongue and his thoughts, eliminating any wish to speak, to deepen the secret of this strange encounter. It was dreamlike; the previous encounters had been nightmarish. That was all. He would find out what it all meant later. For now, he preferred to let the silence, the slowness wash over him. Francesca was looking at him again, as if from a great distance, with a strangely gentle smile. He let the oars dangle at the sides of the boat and smiled back. This time, he was not trying to trap a girl with his quick words and witty jokes. He was caught in a trap of silence.

In the heavy air, the electrical tension increased a degree.

Mario had grabbed the oars and was roaming through fog so dense they could barely see 20 meters from the boat.

Suddenly, he stared at the white fog and exclaimed, "The dam!"

A dark mass emerged from the fog. At the same time, he heard a deep rumble. The boat started to change course.

"A sluice valve!" he thought, his throat tight. "One or more sluice valves have opened. We're going to crash against the gates!"

He rowed furiously, trying to go back, but whirlpools started to form.

"We'll never make it!" he shouted to Francesca, his voice hoarse, as if someone were strangling him.

In a brief, shocking vision, he saw a serene face, smiling. She didn't understand the danger! She didn't know that the valves had opened suddenly, to start up certain turbines... It was too late—and there was no point—to show her the danger of death soaring above them.

As he rowed with all his might, the boat slid into a whirlpool and capsized.

When Mario regained consciousness, he was coughing, suffocating. He was lying face down on the bottom of the overturned boat, spewing up water he had swallowed.

Finally, air entered his lungs normally. He must have inhaled only a small amount of water. Lifting himself up on his elbows, he looked around.

The overturned boat was floating, bobbing gently on a small wave under a blinding sun. Abruptly, he remembered the woman.

"Francesca!" he shouted.

He coughed, then uttered a desperate exclamation. She had drowned. He had escaped death alone. No doubt, his grip on the boast had been firmer... A short while later, the sluice valves closed as suddenly as they had opened and the boat had not reached the gates protecting the turbines. It started to drift toward the shore.

Mario turned his head and peered. Thirty meters from the shore a group of peasants stood in a tight cluster, motionless and silent.

"Francesca!" he shouted. "She was with me! We have to search for her right away! Help me!"

In response, one of the men bent down, apparently looking for something.

The stone struck the water two meters away from Mario.

CHAPTER VII

The peasants rumbled like a pack of wolves. Marios expected them to all start howling together. Two more stones flew through the air.

"Between Scylla and Charybdis..." murmured Mario.

"You're crazy!" he shouted.

Just then, something moved through group of men. Three women were approaching, walking along the path that led to the village. One of them, whose enormous hips rolled with each step, raised her arms and spoke loudly. From the distance, Mario recognized the innkeeper. She had recognized him as well, since she pointed him out to the others with a gesture that could pass for a plea. Mario caught a few words here and there.

"It's a guy from Naples..." she said. "He got here last evening... He has nothing to do with our problems."

"He's got no business here!" exclaimed a large man with a dark, bearded face.

"It's all right, he can make do," said another, shrugging. "He's large enough to..."

Mario did not hear the end of the sentence. The peasants were dispersing like theater goers at the end of a show. The journalist used his hands to paddle to the shore.

The innkeeper had stayed behind on her own, watching his efforts coldly. When he reached shore, she took a step ahead and said, "You didn't complete your hotel form."

Mario howled like a dog and shrugged in disgust.

"She drowned, no doubt…" he replied.

"What?" asked the woman.

"I'm talking about a girl who was on this boat."

He grabbed the woman by the shoulders and shook her.

"You're all a pack of savages here!" he shouted in her face. "When someone is in danger, no one comes to help you. Just the opposite. You throw stones at them to hasten their end."

He let her go and turned his head away.

"Since…" he murmured. "With no diving gear…"

The sun was very high. The boat had capsized in the early hours of the morning. What hope was there?

"What's this about a girl?" asked the innkeeper, scowling.

"Her name is…"

He shrugged, bitterly, and continued, "Her name was Francesca da Ricci."

The woman frowned, saying, "There's no one here by that name. You let all this nonsense go. You'll have problems if you tell lies…"

"Lies!" shouted Mario, losing control

"Whatever…" interrupted the woman. "The villagers aren't interested in your stories about girls. This morning the church was ransacked."

She looked down at him and said, "I wonder what time you left your room."

Mario realized there was no point in talking about his nocturnal outing. He would immediately be blamed for all of the destruction committed during the night. Well, perhaps not by Benedetto and Angelina who knew what was going on... But the farmers did not associate with the villagers...

"Don't even ask." Mario replied, dryly. "Your hotel is not a boarding school. As for all the rest, you should know that I'm a journalist and I won't keep my position at the newspaper for long if I focus my reports on church vandalism."

The innkeeper looked away.

"Fine, fine…" she said, walking away.

Mario caught up with her and said, "I could care less about what happened to your church but my trade requires me to investigate. I would prefer to leave a village where the villagers don't help people immediately…"

He kicked a pebble with the tip of his shoe. Water squelched in his shoe.

"What exactly did happen?" he asked, in an arrogant tone, as if he were granting her some concession by questioning her.

Because of her trade, the innkeeper was a little more civil than the other villagers. She fell into his trap.

"Someone broke the stained-glass windows…" she said. "And some things inside."

They walked on together and soon reached the first few houses.

"Everything that was broken or damaged came, apparently from the old church."

"The old church?"

"The one in the old village that's now covered by the artificial lake."

Mario did not respond. He thought about what Benedetto had said, specifically about the old village. Events seemed to take place in keeping with some bizarre plan that seemed to have something to do with the old buildings now standing under 20 meters of water.

And what about the woman's voice he'd heard near the dam? Instinctively, Mario connected that memory with Francesca. He knew that something had been triggered in his thoughts when the woman in the boat had invited him to accompany her. He had refused to accept that consciously at the time. Francesca's appearance was already strange enough, without connecting her to the nocturnal voice... if he had it would all have turned into some sort of unsettling fairy tale.

Now, Mario could not stand up against his own thoughts.

But he ended up wondering if the fatal boat ride had even taken place. While half asleep had he actually climbed on a boat that capsized in the lake? Had he perhaps fallen back to sleep and dreamed? Francesca was gradually losing the thin layer of reality his memory had clothed her in. The thought of searching for the body of a drowning victim who had never existed was growing more and more absurd. Mario preferred to view Francesca as a character in a dream since, otherwise, she was just as lost to him, but in a much more sinister manner.

He turned his thoughts back to what the innkeeper had said.

"What does the priest have to say about it?" he asked.

"He's only coming tomorrow. He takes care of several parishes."

"Has the police been notified?"

"How?"

"By telephone maybe?"

"The line is down... The storm no doubt..."

"No one went to Olmeto?"

"No bus today."

Irritated, Mario decided not to ask if anyone in the village had a bicycle.

"I'll go," he said.

The woman turned to look at him, grumbling, "On your Lambretta?

He stared at her.

"Of course!" he said.

"It's been destroyed."

Mario jumped.

"What are you saying?" he shouted.

She shrugged then grumbled, "I wondered if you had something to do with everything that happened... Then I saw that your motorcycle had been damaged. No doubt it was the people who vandalized the church."

They walked through the village. Mario abandoned the innkeeper and strode off ahead of her. He was trembling with rage.

He found his scooter where he had left it in the shed. The gas tank was riddled with holes, that looked as if they had been made by some kind of punch. The gas had flowed out and the shed was filled with a violent stench. He bent down to look. The tires had been slashed. The spare tire as well.

But the strangest thing was the rust that streaked the paint.

Devastated, Mario stepped out of the shed and ran into the innkeeper.

"You should have provided a door and a lock!" he shouted.

She shrugged and said, "Travelers who don't like my inn can go elsewhere. You should have taken better precautions. I won't keep you from getting stoned a second time."

Mario bit his lower lip, furious.

"I'll be more than pleased to leave this place!" he grumbled. "But I don't see myself pushing my scooter kilometers and kilometers with flat tires. I'll have to stay here until I find some way to get to Olmeto for repairs. Does anyone here have a car?"

"The doctor."

"That's perfect. I'll dismantle the tank and the wheels and I'll ask the doctor to take me to the city with my stuff."

"Good luck!" she said over her shoulder. "The sooner you leave, the better. Journalists attract various things."

Mario walked into the small common room in the hotel. A scrawny young waitress that he had not had the opportunity to see the previous evening was wringing a filthy rag over a bucket of dirty water. She glanced at Mario who felt slightly uncomfortable. The girl had a mild squint that focused her eyes in an unexpected direction.

"You didn't eat breakfast," she said in a sharp, grating voice.

She had uttered those words in a satisfied tone and Mario almost expected her to add "And that's fine with me."

After a moment, he replied, "No... and I'm hungry."

"I can make you an omelet with ham and cheese..." she shouted. "And rice."

Why was she shouting like that? She was standing two meters away from him, with her rag dripping on her bare feet.

Mario clenched his jaws, then said "Fine," he said. "But wash your hands."

176

She laughed without replying, then disappeared into a greasy kitchen. Mario sat down at the table and started to think about the situation. Everything seemed to indicate that someone or something wanted to keep him in Santa Croce. What was the point of the vandalism to his Lambretta since he had come here on his own?

And there was more: the extraordinary character wearing the hood.... and everything else. Particularly the voice at the lake and the memory of Francesca. It created a sort of singular bewitchment that made the invisible chain solid.

"I haven't left here yet," thought Mario, feeling unsettled.

The waitress brought the plates to him, chuckling silently.

While Mario attacked the omelet, the waitress stood a few steps away, following his every move with an indiscretion that seemed both stupid and malicious. He looked at the girl's hands. It was obvious that she had not even dipped them in clean water. But what could he say? The damage was done and Mario was too hungry to refuse to eat the eggs even though he was certain that he would find mud and broom bristles in them.

"I've seen things..." the servant declared after a moment.

She had lowered her voice while talking. Mario put his fork down.

"Yes?" he said.

"He did a good job on your Lambretta..." she observed, sounding satisfied.

"Who do you mean by *he*?"

She turned to look at the door to the inn which stood open and said, "The penitent.

Mario jumped.

"You saw him last night?"

Her lips stretched in a thin smile and she squinted at the side of Mario's head.

"I was standing behind my window. He went into the shed. He had a dagger in his hand."

A dagger! How absurd! Yet, those holes… the ones that looked as if they had been made by a punch...

"A penitent armed with a dagger…" repeated Mario. "You do realize that sounds ridiculous, don't you?

"He didn't look ridiculous," she said, seriously. "It was strange… some sort of monk carrying a blade in his hand, a blade that shone in the moonlight…"

If Mario had not seen the same type of character with his own eyes on the road to Santa Croce, he would have simply shrugged. But they had both seen the same thing.

"Something bad is about to happen," she whispered to him, nodding her head with conviction.

She jiggled as she moved about, as if listening to some inner music.

"Some are going to lose a lot!" she added. "Maybe even their lives!"

She picked up her bucket with a bark of laughter and disappeared back into the kitchen. Mario swallowed his last mouthful of omelet painfully.

Was she retarded? Her words were certainly upsetting... But weren't people like that often clairvoyant, able to see the future...?

"Enough!" grumbled Mario.

He pulled the plate of rice, peppers and tomatoes closer and cut two slices of cheese.

He was finding it harder and harder to eat.

The waitress reappeared, approached, gave him a cross-eyed glance and declared, "Bad things have already started happening."

Mario shrugged.

"Vandalism..." he said.

"Vand... a... lism?" repeated the girl. "I don't know about that. One thing I do know for sure is the bambino."

Mario stared at her and repeated "The bambino?"

"Down there, in the shacks."

Mario perked his ears up.

"Yes?" he said.

"He's sick."

Mario immediately made the connection between the beggar and the woman with the candelabra. The child was sick. Was that why the mother had reacted so brutally to the vagabond?

Mario recalled Benedetto's words, particularly the story about the goats.

He put his fork down.

CHAPTER VIII

The road wound, yellow and naked under the pewter clouds.

A pebble rolled under Mario's feet. Why that one and not another? That represented one of the unpredictable paths of destiny. What was destiny in Santa Croce? Pebbles rolling here and there converging on a single point. A future point. A foreseeable future where the fabric of the setting could tear with the unbearable screeching of things dying...

Mario had been given directions to the doctor's house. It stood a few hundred meters from the village, on a stoney, inhospitable site on the slopes of Monte Peccatore. Mario saw it in the distance, a white cube devoid of any architectural artifice, surrounded by skillfully maintained greenery.

He walked to the small gate and rang the bell. He rang the bell firmly, with determination. Since getting involved in this obscure matter, he felt his trade growing strong and stronger within himself. How could he become a true journalist when he only covered musty old affairs devoid of interest? Now, despite the ridiculous events that had initially brought him here, something unusual was being woven through the lightning. That encouraged serious investigation.

Only one thing could take his newfound strength from him: the memory of Francesca never left him. The face with the black eyes remained in the background behind every gesture he made, like shadows follow movements.

A woman walked down the steps of the square house. She walked to the gate, smoothly and quickly. Mario felt the world spin around him... It was Francesca da Ricci.

The journalist quickly recovered his self-control. He bowed with a forced smile as she opened the gate.

"What do you want?" the young woman asked coldly, standing a meter away from him.

This startled him. What game was she playing?

"I was going to ask Dr. Casciattelli to help me out of a bad situation," he said. "But your presence here surprises me..."

She stared at him.

"How does my presence here surprise you? We don't know one another. To whom do I have the honor?"

He shook his head. Things were getting murkier and murkier.

"Have you forgotten that we met this morning and that the boat capsized? You're not prepared to explain how you got away..." he asked gently.

Francesca blinked several times, as if making a painful mental effort.

"Come in, then," she said. "I don't know what you're talking about... but my uncle, Dr. Casciattelli, may be able to help you. I expect him back soon."

She walked ahead of him.

"Would it be of interest to you to know that I know your name? That you're Francesca da Ricci?" asked Mario.

She turned back. The surprise on her face seemed genuine.

"That's right!" she said.

"Then I'll introduce myself to you a second time," he said. "Mario Salgari. That name means nothing to you?"

She stopped on the steps to the porch and looked at him sadly.

"There's something I try to keep hidden from myself," she said. "I suffer from a memory disorder. And when the attacks occur, I have no awareness of the information people give me. I think you're sincere. So, I must have had a new attack today."

She looked at the ground and seemed to be making a great effort to search through her memory.

"No," she finally said. "I don't know what I did this morning."

She took a step down in his direction and said in a low voice, "Will you forgive me?"

Once again, she had that strange expression on her face, so deeply moving, as she had had during their boat ride, which seemed barely real at this point. He clenched his jaws.

"Of course."

He moved to take her hand. She moved back briskly, walked up the last few stairs and pushed the front door open.

"Come in then," she said. "I don't think you'll have to wait long."

The parlor bore the mark of a strong personality. The decoration revealed excellent taste and a clear tendency towards the exotic which was all the more surprising when contrasted with the poverty and isolation of the region.

They sat facing one another in gigantic chairs with primitive shapes that must come from the other side of the world, although Mario was incapable of identifying exactly where.

"Your uncle seems to have travelled a lot," he observed after a moment of silence.

She glanced at a display of Polynesian weapons.

"Yes, a great deal," she said, nodding. "But I only see him rarely and my... my memory problem prevents me from talking about it with any accuracy..."

After a moment, she said, "They brought me here in a car three days ago. I need absolute rest, both physical and mental. This region is calm."

Mario thought he heard veiled irony behind those words. He said nothing about it, but his mind started to wander. No, the region was not at all calm. In a harsh yet simple setting, it hid a mystery that did not seem to fit in with normal, daily phenomena. Something diabolical was prowling through the underbrush and along the shores of the lake. Thinking about the lake, Mario involuntarily compared it to a large glassy eye open in the hollow of the mountains, glancing in concern at a sky that was constantly filled with lightning.

"I go out from time to time..." she continued. "That way the time passes pleasantly."

She looked at him and suddenly grew animated.

"But, fortunately, I don't lose the memory of everything I do. If I have lost my memory of my outing this morning, which you say ended tragically..."

"You must be a good swimmer," he said, interrupting her.

She smiled, obviously in response to some personal reference that she had no intention of telling him about and replied, "Fairly good."

She shook her dark curls, then continued, "But as for my outings I have a perfect recollection of the large

Venetto abbey. A splendid piece of architecture. Did I see it yesterday? Or the day before?"

Something clicked in Mario's mind. The Venetto abbey? What did that mean? That monument had been completely destroyed by an earthquake at the beginning of the 18th century...

"Are you... Are you sure about what you're saying?" Mario asked hesitantly.

"Yes, yes," she replied immediately. "I found it very striking!"

Mario felt uncomfortable, thinking "Obviously, if I had recently visited a monument that had been destroyed two centuries ago without a trace, I would find that memory rather striking too."

She was lying. Gratuitously. Like she had no doubt lied about the boat ride— and her so-called amnesia.

He had to question everything she said. Gratuitous lies? Really? A mythomaniac? Could he be certain of that? Mario was not far from believing that this fabric of pure inventions had, for some secret reason, something to do with the unusual series of minor events that took place in hiding each night in Santa Croce. Why? He'd manage to figure things out...

Outside the sky was growing dark. Through the large, open window, Mario and Francesca could see heavy masses of clouds rising at the horizon to attack the sky. The sun had already disappeared and the silent moisture of a new storm was insinuating itself into the gloomy immobility of the landscape. Mario through he saw an expression of concern cross quickly over Francesca's face, an expression she tried to hide with a tense smile. She launched into an enthusiastic description of the Venetto abbey and Mario lost it.

She must really have seen the abbey. She provided details that could not be made up and her account was so clear... Her depiction brought conviction and Mario did not knew which saint he should dedicate himself to.

High in the sky thunder rolled and echoed for a long time, bouncing from the black clouds to the steep mountains, from the mountains to the valley, from the valley to the lead-colored sky. Francesca leapt up suddenly, then forced herself to adopt a more dignified posture. But the expression on her face revealed a panic that was completely disproportionate to the danger represented by the storm. Of course, many people are afraid of lightning... others experience the electrical tension in the atmosphere as a painful nervous imbalance... But her reaction was excessive!

She headed over to the window and closed it quickly. Then she started to pace about the room. Mario was concerned for her.

A painful silence reigned over the room for a few minutes. Suddenly, purple light filled the room, followed by an ear-shattering thunderclap that shook the house from top to bottom. The lighting had struck nearby.

With a cry, Francesca took refuge in the middle of the parlor. Leaning against the back of a large chair, she hid her face in her hands as her entire body trembled. Mario got up and headed toward her. But she immediately backed away, holding her arms outstretched. He recalled how she had backed away on the porch when he had tried to hold her hand. What was this new exaggerated defense reflex? She could not seriously think he intended take advantage of her fear of the storm to attack her in her uncle's house?

He stepped back, distraught, concerned. The rain, an extraordinarily dense rain, started pounding violently against the windows. Francesca gradually regained her self-control. Standing a few meters from Mario, she looked at him intensely, as if she were desperate to refuse the consolation and the moral support he was offering to her.

"I'm… I'm sorry," she said in a quavering voice.

She made a great effort to continue.

"You have no idea how pleased I am to accept your sympathy… but you can't do anything for me… Quite the contrary… I'm the one who may well place you in danger."

"What do you mean?"

"That's how it is. You must not be near me when a thunderstorm is threatening."

His eyes grew wide, then he frowned.

"What do you mean?"

She was clenching and unclenching her hands convulsively.

"Don't try to understand. I can't tell you anything else. I'm just warning you. Please leave me alone. You can come back to see my uncle once the danger has disappeared."

"The danger?"

"Yes, yes! Come back when you want. I'll always be pleased to see you… But for now, leave. Leave right away. Do you see? The storm is getting worse!"

Mario shook his head, upset by this behavior. "She's unbalanced," he thought. "Seriously unbalanced. Mythomaniac, anxious… What a pity… Such a beautiful girl!"

"That's fine…" he said. "But I'll get drenched!"

"That's not important. You'll dry. It's very warm. You won't be in any danger… Less so than by staying here."

She opened the door.

"Goodbye... Mario. Come back. I'll tell my uncle you dropped by."

A new thunderclap made her leap back.

"Hurry up!" she said. Mario walked past her. He stepped out into a veritable warm shower on the porch that blurred his vision immediately as the door slammed closed behind him.

"What hospitality!" he grumbled, making his way through the garden toward the gate.

He waded through puddles on the road. The slope of the terrain created streams here and there, draining the rain toward ditches, uncovering the stone. His mind swirling with extravagant hypotheses, Mario, set out under the warm rain accompanied by the roiling clouds in the sky and the pale flashes of lightning.

CHAPTER IX

Back at the inn, Mario shut himself up in his room and changed his clothing. On his way in he had asked the waitress for a glass of boiling chianti, an unusual order the stupid girl seemed to find hilarious. Yet, she brought the drink to him and it was so hot after the storm he was unable to drink it.

"I have to get my mind straight about this," he said to himself.

He took a tourist guide for the Olmeto region from his suitcase. Very quickly, he verified the accuracy of what he had been thinking. The Venetto abbey had been destroyed by an earthquake in Calabria and Sicily, in 1732. At least that was the opinion of the author of the guide who had collected the information from oral tradition. Historically, there was no mention in any work of an earthquake at that place and at the time... What was certain was that the Venetto abbey had been destroyed 235 years ago. The only time it was mentioned was with respect to the religious life of the South or to clarify certain battles portrayed in several paintings and sculptures that could be seen in Olmeto.

Mario sat on the side of his bed for a moment, meditating. Obviously, Francesca had lied. But with such sincerity, with such striking details! She made lying an art form.

Mario shrugged. Every time he thought about Francesca he ran into a brick wall. Who exactly was she? Was she actually Dr. Casciattelli's niece? Or some mental patient he was treating in his home? Or both? All in all, she'd never claimed to be anything else...

But what about the voice he'd heard at the lake, from the top of the parapet? Was it hers? And if it were, how could the physician let someone so unbalanced take nocturnal boat rides on the lake where she might easily be drowned or broken against the gates protecting the turbines?

Mario found it difficult to accept the idea of neurosis or even madness. The young girl had made such a strong impression on him that, when he saw her in the doctor's garden, he had experienced a joy disproportionate to what he should have felt when meeting someone who was a virtual stranger.

And then there was something else. Whether he wanted it or not, he had to admit to himself that, when he had left the house in the rain storm, he'd had the impression that he was escaping from some grave danger. Did that danger exist and what was it really? Was there any connection with the repulsive apparitions and the acts of vandalism? It seemed to him that he was being held in Santa Croce not only by the damage to his vehicle but also by some sort of bewitchment...

He stood up and swore in fury. Look at what he'd gotten into! He had set out to prepare a miserable report on some petty larcenies and now he was struggling with foolish ideas. And for some reason or another, he was really stuck, isolated in a village of primitive savages where incomprehensible events were taking place.

Low on the horizon, the sun was providing very little heat, particularly since the clouds had not entirely left the sky and the storm, a short distance off, seemed about to return at any moment and attack the village yet again.

The roads had either swallowed up all of the water that had fallen recently or it had partially evaporated. Mario made a short detour to take a look at the lake before continuing his way up the mountain. He met a man at a crossroads.

A grotesque character wearing an elegant yet scruffy suit. He was walking in Mario's direction, waving his arms about and singing a bawdy song. Then he fell silent and shook his fist at someone behind him on the deserted road.

The right pocket on his jacket was pulled down by some heavy object. Mario recognized a flask.

The man did not seem to notice Mario's presence until he came right up to him. then he stopped short, stumbled a bit, and stared the journalist up and down.

"Nice shit!" he yelled in the journalist's face. Mario stepped back, overcome by the powerful stench of alcohol.

The man fell silent for a moment, wobbled back and forth, then right to left.

"To top it all off, they did that!" he said, suddenly.

"Who..." said Mario, in a conciliatory tone. "Who did?"

The man glanced at him, looking semi lucid.

"Who?" he repeated. "If I tell you, you won't believe me. So, there's no point insisting, is there?"

He clenched his fist and brandished it at the lake again. Although the man was quite drunk, Mario found his behavior intriguing, even disturbing. Once again, the lake played a role. It played a role in the drunk's words and gestures, just as it had in the case of Benedetto. The journalist hoped to obtain more information this time.

"My name is Mario Salgari and I'm a journalist with the *Corriere di Napoli*. To whom do I have the honor of addressing?"

"Honor?" he said. "Your honor won't earn you a conversation with me..."

He let his arms drop to his sides and stared at the ground in front of his feet, as if overwhelmed by some sudden discouragement.

"Who am I?" he asked. "A hasty question... Before you know *who* I am, you must first know *if* I am... if I exist... and for how long. The thing..."

He started to babble, slapped his pocket, then said, "The thing is infinitely more important. With these horrors..."

He tipped his chin in the direction of the lake.

"What horrors?" Mario said gently.

The man shook his head.

"There's no point..." he said with great difficulty. "You won't find out anything... You would do well to return to Naples. Here, life is an integral part of death and we end up wondering if we're on one side or the other."

Mario frowned. He did not understand anything the man said, but he did think that the sententious stammering dictated by the alcohol hid some terrible truth. As the character turned to look at the lake with a gesture that combined anger and fear, Mario noticed a detail: the drunk man had only one ear. Where the left ear should have been, there was a star-shaped scar.

"Signor! Signor!" shouted Mario.

But the other man was no longer listening. He was stumbling on his way, singing, chortling and cursing.

The journalist swiped his forehead with his hand. He was both confused and furious.

"I'll go back to the hotel," he decided. "I'll get what I need to take photos. With each passing hour, I get more information or at least the echoes of some event that fits into my investigation. If I encounter one of those disgusting apparitions, I want palpable proof of it."

He turned about and raced off in the direction of the hotel.

CHAPTER X

By the time Mario left the village, the sun had long vanished behind the mountains. In the strange orangish light that had bathed his conversation with the drunken man, waves of blue shadows slowly washed over the depths of the valleys.

The young got his bearings easily, under the baleful and disapproving eye of a peasant who was carefully placing his tools in a small barn. He headed in the direction of Monte Peccatore, giving no thought to the comments people would make about him that evening.

He quickly found himself in darkness. To the west, clumps of thick clouds were hiding the deep indigo sky here and there and the moon, which had risen early, cast an almost permanent light over the bushes

As he walked, Mario worked at trying to connect the various pieces of information he had managed to garner. The elderly farmer's revelations, which had caused both humor and concern, would perhaps assume their true value if compared to his encounters with Francesca, the drunken man... But no matter which way he looked the journalist was unable to develop an overview or explanation. The most recent elements—Francesca and the drunk—remained outside... as if parallel.

As he had done the first time he went to the farm, the previous night, Mario stopped, listening to the rustling of the wind and insects through the vegetation for a certain sliding sound that seemed to have another cause.

He stood still for a long time without being able to confirm that the noise had been repeated. Yet he had the hateful impression that a troupe of people was milling around him, hidden from sight by a simple curtain of bushes, walking in the same direction as he was. He thought of safaris making their way through dense virgin forests surrounded and accompanied by a silent horde of savages waiting for the right time and place to initiate a surprise attack...

He continued cautiously on his way. He did not know if his fleeting impressions had any concrete reality... but felt that he was surrounded by people in home-spun robes.

He shivered, then complimented himself for bravely stepping into a scrubland at night where anything could appear at any time...

"You do have to keep your morale up in difficult circumstances," he thought. "The fact that I'm brave will help me to grow even braver..."

In the distance ahead of him he thought he heard the sound of a dead branch breaking. He stopped short, heart pounding. But he quickly forgot the cracking of the branch as another sound, a lower one, came from behind him. Rapid breathing, like a creature being chased through the forest by a pack.

He threw himself against the trunk of a pine, hugging it. A few meters away, something heavy was rushing through the foliage, panting like a bellows. It moved away quickly and suddenly, as if the creature that had just rushed past had been some messenger or some laggard delayed by a large troupe. In the distance feet trampled the ground, hoarse voices called out.

His throat dry, Mario stepped out from the precarious shelter provided by the tree, determined to follow the sound that was moving toward the mountain. What was it? A group of peasants beating their way through the vegetation, looking for the vandals of the previous evening? Mario would have liked that to be the explanation. But there was little chance of that. The strange creatures that haunted the night, hidden by homespun hoods?

A cry rang out, bringing him to a stop. The cry rang out behind him, long, sharp, piercing through the night like a blade. Mario realized someone was in danger. Despite the shadows, he raced back along the path he had just covered.

Despite the noise caused by his own race, he knew he was being followed. Or perhaps someone was coming to his aid? No. A woman had been attacked down there, not far from the lake, and those who were racing down the slope behind Mario were no doubt coming as reinforcements for her...

A root caught his foot and he fell to the ground, rolling. Pain shot up his arm. He stood up. The case he was carrying strapped to his back, was bouncing against his hip, hampering his movements. As he ran, Mario recalled something the old farmer had said.

Benedetto had said, "When I pointed my flashlight at his hood, he screamed."

Barely slowing, Mario reached into the case where he had placed his camera before setting out. A new cry rang out, closer this time. Mario stopped to get his bearings. Behind a cluster of pine trees, the glooming expanse of the lake reflected a moon devoured by black clouds. He raced past a curtain of junipers as the cries rang out over and over.

There, on a small rocky outcrop, a white shape crouched down, screaming. Several shadows surrounded it, advancing slowly toward it.

Mario stopped, slowly raising his camera to eye level.

"Let's hope it works!" he thought.

He realized just how revolting his attitude might appear to an uninformed observer: he was taking a photo instead of helping the victim!

There was a flash, followed by screams. The attackers vanished into the bushes, panicked. There, they ran into those who had raced past Mario on the slope and a great uproar took place in the dark.

With a few steps, the journalist reached the white shape lying and moaning on the ground. A final beam of light from the moon revealed the face of Angelina, Benedetto's daughter...

"Quick!" he said, taking her by the arm. "We have to flee. There are too many of them…"

Behind them, the troupe seemed to be reorganizing. The clouds had finished their invasion of the sky and thick shadows covered everything. The lake reflected no light whatsoever. Mario heard breathing approaching through the night.

"Be quick… to the village… it's closer!" Mario panted.

Angelina followed docilely behind him.

But they were surrounded.

Mario recognized that electrical charge that flashed throughout the valley. His nerves were on edge, increasing his fear, making it impossible for him to properly assess their chances of escaping.

His rescue attempt had failed. All he had done was place two people in danger instead of one... It was obvious that the hostile shadows surrounded them, waiting ahead of them, behind them, on all sides.

"Let's try to get past them," Mario murmured.

He grabbed her hand tightly and set out with her to slip between two groups whose locations he had managed to identify somewhat. They managed to do just that. During their mad dash, Mario had violently run into a tree trunk, tearing the skin of his hand and his face on the thorns of a bush. A cry from Angelina revealed that she had suffered the same fate...

Behind them, their pursuers were organizing when a flash of lightning tore through the sky. Rain, a new downpour, immediately fell down on the trees. Shouts rang out through the darkness. Water flowed. The fugitives stopped, listening. And suddenly, a burning, pink, stem of fire connected the clouds and the ground, as a deafening rumble of thunder struck them like a cannonball. They opened their dazzled eyes and they both exclaimed at the same time. A few dozen meters away, flames engulfed a petrified human shape, sparks shooting high in the sky. It looked like a fireworks display.

In a concert of terrified screams, the beings that had been pursuing them reached the lake, followed by the sound of bodies diving into the water.

"Frogs!" exclaimed Mario, in a failed attempt to make a joke.

But Angelina had fallen to the ground in a faint.

Angelina's was not unconscious for long. The downpour revived her. Mario got up and stood over her, to protect her face from the large drops of rain.

Angelina stood up painfully, supported by Mario.

"Oh!" she said. "It was good of you to come and..."

She interrupted what she had been about to say with a small cry. She had caught sight of the flame consuming a misshapen blob. Hiding her face in the young man's shoulder, she moaned in fear.

"It's horrible…" she stammered.

Mario caressed her hair. Water dripped from both of their heads.

"Give me a minute," he said. "Don't be afraid, I won't leave you behind."

She clung to him.

"Don't leave me alone," she said, her voice quavering.

He released her grasp gently.

"I'm going to get a closer look.. " he explained.

He set out and his limping gait revealed that, apart from the emotional consequences, he had also felt the effects of the lightning that had struck so close to them both. Thinking about it, he was surprised that he had not been thrown to the ground.

The shape struck by the lightning had acted in some way like a lightning rod…

Seen at close hand, in the light case by the last few sparks, it was impossible to make out anything other than a small heap of damp ashes that cast a nauseating odor over the night.

The storm was waning. It was a fleeting storm, like those that continuously attacked the region. Mario had to admit that it had occurred just in time to get them out of a bad situation.

He decided to accompany Angelina back to the farm. With the storm threatening to return at any minute, a new encounter with the hostile shapes was most unlikely. That was why he decided to accompany her to the farm and not the village.

Along the way, he filed this new adventure, which cast the farmer's convictions in a morbid light, with the evidence he already had obtained from his investigation.

The shadows could represent any group of evil-doers, determined to terrorize the region... but this flash of lightning had transformed one of them into a torch... that took the entire matter into a very direct zone, one that was radically monstrous and inexplicable.

"Bah!" said Mario. "Anyone can get hit by lightning."

Yes... but what human body burned like that, as if it had been made of saltpeter...? And what person, fleeing from the lightning, would have thrown themselves into the water, *without reappearing or returning to shore...?*

He did not tell Angelina about these unsettling thoughts, knowing in advance that she would have said, "My father thinks..."

Like lightning emerging from the clouds, a blinding connection appeared in Mario's mind: *why had Francesca been so afraid of the storm?*

CHAPTER XI

Guided by the barking of the dogs, Mario approached the farm. Angelina, still suffering from the effects of her faint, was finding it difficult to find her way, despite the moonlight shining through a large hole in the clouds.

Soon, he saw the light in the common room. Behind the fence, a voice ordered the dogs to be quiet.

Then it said, "Is that you, Angelina?"

The young girl started to run, calling for her father, who opened the door in the fence. He hugged his daughter, who launched into a series of explanations, "Mr. Mario accompanied me," she said. "He saved me... I was chased by the... by the evil ones!"

"Good grief!" shouted Benedetto, turning to Mario.

Mario looked at the table Angelina had set. She had placed a plate there with an omelet and peppers while Benedetto, his face more wrinkled than ever, had produced a bottle of Frascati, in its wicker packaging. His daughter went out then returned with goat cheese and a plate of tagliatelle.

Come, son," said Benedetto. "You can do the honors."

He pointed at the meal. Mario sat down at the table with a smile and the conversation, which had been interrupted briefly, started back up.

Mario had already learned that the enraged, drunken man he had encountered was none other than the doctor. He now understood the reasons for the man's rage. The doctor had gone to see the baby the waitress at the inn had mentioned, the baby Mario had seen in its mother's arms, the previous night... the baby who had fallen strangely ill after being rocked by... by one the mysterious, repugnant creatures.

What struck Mario about that revelation was that Dr. Casciattelli had seemed, with his words, to seriously incriminate those the mother had accused.

"Of course!" Benedetto replied when Mario told him that.

"When I told you that the doctor would find a very simple explanation... but that he too was well aware of the truth..."

The farmer then compared that sinister contamination with the ailment his goat had suffered. He also compared the doctor's mutilation to the print he had discovered... So much so that Mario, in turn, wondered if the doctor knew more about the situation than anyone else.

During the meal, Benedetto spoke about the mysterious voice Mario had heard at the lake.

"Did that damned voice sing again?" he asked with a grimace of disgust.

"No, no..." Mario said, pensively.

He could not get the memory of Francesca out of his mind, and was constantly connecting it with the invisible singer, although he had never identified the two voices. He was going to speak to Benedetto about the boat trip on the lake, about the boat capsizing, about his conversation with Francesca at the doctor's house...

As he thought about all this, he asked himself an absurd question for the first time: was Francesca actually Dr. Casciattelli's niece... or did she come out of the lake at night to...

To contaminate those she encountered? Like the "beggar woman"? Mario shivered as he thought about how *Francesca had moved away* when he had tried to hug her...

The meal had ended and Benedetto thanked Mario for the tenth time. The were seated face to face, with the traditional bottle of maraschino liqueur between them as the spicy perfume of the damp scrub wafted in through the open window.

Benedetto allowed himself to wax melancholic over his favorite topic: the old village.

"There was so much misfortune," he said.

"What do you mean?" asked Mario.

The old man waved his hand evasively, saying, "In the old days, wars, prisons, slavery, illness... Perhaps it was the same all over Italy, perhaps elsewhere as well... but from what people told me the old village had more than its share. And I wonder if all that suffering penetrated the old stone, like coffee soaks into a sugar cube. That's it! Houses filled with misfortune, misfortune coating the walls... Walls that radiate evil like fire radiates heat!"

"Here he goes again with his tall tales," thought Mario. But he no longer felt he was in a good position to judge the old man. Logic and skepticism were losing their weight considering all of the abnormal events he had witnessed.

Mario was surprised when he caught himself glancing in concern out the open window. The dogs were quiet... But somewhere in the valley, shadows were no doubt lurking now that the storm was no longer threatening...

When he looked back at the old farmer, he saw that Benedetto was also looking in the direction of the window, at the black rectangle where the light cast by the lamp pierced a hole through the courtyard, vanishing, powerless, after struggling with the shadows for a few meters.

The conversation continued in this manner for a long time, taking such strange turns that Mario found himself falling into a ghostly universe, halfway between dream and reality, where monstrosity was the norm pushing normal reality out of its way. Rocked by the old man's words, Mario gave into the fatigue of the past 24 hours and, without realizing it, he slipped into an invincible drowsiness.

The dream, the dream that came from the edge of his consciousness, overshadowing messages from the real world... How long did it last? A second? A quarter of an hour? His eyes half closed, Mario suddenly found himself both in the old man's home and somewhere else at the same time. An elsewhere that was distant in time and space. Where he belonged to a different, implacable world for a moment.

He found himself in a vast clearing where the heat was stifling. Men were standing around him. Like them, he was wearing a prison uniform. Based on the temperature and the dense vegetation, he decided he was somewhere in the tropics. He also knew the year was 1890.

What crime had he committed to deserve prison? He had no idea and felt no guilt. Yet he was part of a group that the prison guard had placed around a large scaffold that stood in the middle of the clearing.

The ranks opened to murmurs and insults. A prisoner surrounded by six armed men walked toward the scaffold. At the other side of the clearing, a herculean man appeared, carrying an axe on his shoulder. At that point, Mario noticed the chopping block on the scaffold. He shivered as terror washed over him, as if he were the convict about to be decapitated.

The man with the axe walked slowly up the few wooden steps, stopped at the chopping block and leaned on the long handle of his axe. Surrounded by guards, the condemned man joined him. His hands were bound behind his back and Mario saw his face for the first time. A face horrifically disfigured by a disease that twisted his features and carved disgusting wounds in his flesh. No nose, a mouth like a crater, an empty eye socket. Mario realized the convicts were infected with leprosy.

Docilely, as if exhausted by the weight of an unbearable existence, the condemned man knelt down and placed his terrifying head on the chopping block. The executioner raised his axe.

With a single motion, the blade fell and the head rolled onto the platform of the scaffold. At the same time, the executioner dropped the instrument of death and raised his hand quickly to his face. He had been splattered with the victim's blood and was rubbing his cheek and eyelid vigorously with the sleeve of his filthy shirt.

Slowly, the convicts swarmed past the guards. They walked toward the scaffold in a threatening mob. Carried along by the crowd, Mario moved ahead with them. The executioner stood up and looked at the men. In the silence, broken only by the sound of their footsteps, Mario saw that lightning-fast leprosy had already attacked the face of the motionless man. His skin was cracking, as if being worked by a colony of internal parasites and was covered with purple sores.

What is the life between us worth
If death loves you?

... a gentle voice sang.

Torn abruptly from his waking dream, Mario leapt up, eyes wide with horror.

Benedetto stood up before he did and reached for his gun. Oddly, the dogs were yelping and whining.

"I dreamed," said Mario, wiping his forehead with his hand.

The old man stopped in front of him and looked at him darkly.

"No," he said. "Is that the voice you heard at the lake?"

Mario took a step toward the window.

"Yes," he murmured. "It's her. It's Francesca."

A frightening vision filled his mind: he saw Francesca being tortured by a disgusting leper, her face slowly decomposing as she continued to sing the same song, in the same gentle, urgent voice.

"Francesca?" asked Benedetto.

"I have to go..." declared Mario. "She's calling me."

Benedetto raised his hand as an expression of fear washed over his face.

"No, son! Don't do that!" he shouted.

Behind him, Angelina appeared, wearing a black coat over her white nightgown, and joined the old man in beseeching the journalist.

But Mario was not listening to them. He walked over to the door and opened it.

"The dogs!" shouted Benedetto.

Mario was already outside in the moonlit courtyard.

CHAPTER XII

Mario walked through the dogs, crossing the courtyard and none of them attacked him. That was a puzzle he had no intention of delving into just then. His mind was elsewhere.

What time was it? Almost one o'clock, according to his wristwatch. Was that time at which the voice usually manifested itself? Since he had heard it through a half sleep filled with nightmares, he could not recall the intensity with which it had resonated in his ears. But he was convinced that it did not come from the lake. That would be impossible since there was close to a kilometer of scrubland between the farm and the reservoir.

This time it had to have come from the side of the mountain, perhaps even the groves of trees that stood ten meters from the farm.

He walked quickly in the direction of lake, propelled into unthinking motion by the connection his mind made between the lake and the voice.

But, when he arrived at the crossroads where he had encountered the doctor, he did not turn in the direction of the lake but toward Dr. Casciattelli's house. It took him some time to admit the truth: the voice, as he had heard when waking, was similar to Francesca's and, in his mind, the young girl was now connected to both the cube-shaped house and the sleeping waters of the lake.

That house was nearby, standing among the pines like a silver block in the moonlight. He thought he heard the weak creaking of a door in the distance. Hampered by the noise of his racing feet, he was unable to determine if someone else was rushing ahead of him through the shadows. But the creaking made him think that someone, who had initially been hiding near the farm, had now reached the house and entered it. If that were so, it was most likely Francesca. And in that case, the young girl and the mermaid at the lake were one and the same. Mario was more and more certain of that.

He walked over to the fence. The house seemed deserted, dead. Mario hesitated. What excuse would he give the doctor if he encountered the man? Some sickness? Why not?

He found the gate closed, but did not ring the bell. The gate opened quietly. Treading carefully, he walked through the overgrown garden. No sound came from the house. No light.

He stopped again on the porch. No, of course, he couldn't go in without announcing his presence. The doctor might think he was a thief...

As he hesitated, the door opened with a slight creak, the same sound he had thought he heard a few moments earlier. A woman stood in the subdued light that flowed through the doorway.

"Come in quickly..." whispered Francesca.

Feeling like a criminal, Mario stepped into the entrance.

"Follow me," said the young girl.

She guided him into a small room that opened off the hallway, at the opposite end from the parlor where she had already entertained him. She entered the room behind him and closed the door.

The room was filled with a gentle, pinkish light, which seemed favorable for the confidences Mario felt he was authorized to solicit...

"So," he said. "You were at the farm..."

She sat down on a low couch, eyes open wide in surprise.

"At the farm…" she repeated. "What farm?"

Mario frowned in disappointment. He realized that he would learn nothing about her activities. Or… was his imagination making him go astray and lose his way in interpretations that had no connection with reality? Tired of battling with enigmas, he went to sit down next to her and changed the subject.

"Does your uncle know I'm here?" he asked.

She shrugged and said, "He sleeps upstairs and, even if he weren't sleeping, he would not be curious about you. I'm allowed to see whoever I want to."

Mario fell silent for a moment. Francesca was certainly not over the age of 18 and families in the south did not tend to give very young girls that kind of freedom. And, after all, the house belonged to Dr. Casciattelli. He could have refused to let any stranger in, despite Francesca's wishes, particularly if that stranger came in the middle of the night…

However, caught up in the fascination that sparkled in Francesca's eyes, Mario abandoned the topic, keeping the questions that it raised in his mind for himself. But the song was something completely different. It concerned him and it most likely concerned Francesca as well.

"I believe that I had heard your voice," he said with a certain amount of conviction.

"Where?" she said, sounding surprised.

"Near the farm where I was earlier," he repeated. "Through an open window, I heard a woman's voice, one that sounded like your voice… singing."

She shook her head, but kept her eyes on the floor.

"I heard that song for the second time... last night..." he added.

He glanced at her sidewise. But she seemed plunged in some inner dream that was barely accessible to words.

Suddenly she looked up and, without commenting on Mario's words, she asked, "Do you believe that one can love several times?"

He stared at her for a moment. If she was hoping to distract him, she had succeeded since, hearing her simple question, he felt even more violently troubled that he had the previous night, at the dam.

"Of course, he finally replied. "Not just anyone... not just any time... but it's not rare... Many people have loved several times over the course of their lives, with the same passion."

"Over the course of their lives..." Francesca repeated in a strange voice.

Without knowing exactly why, Mario connected those words with the incomprehensible excursion Francesca claimed she had made to the Venetto abbey.

The conversation continued for a long time growing more and more abandoned. Francesca was ambiguous, then gentle, then provocative. Mario, gave into her charming wiles without a struggle. He did not for a moment question the sincerity of the feelings Francesca progressively expressed in his regard, feelings he experienced himself with a new force. He had fallen in love with her in the boat and, without him completely realizing it, that passion had been driven by the mystery surrounding the nocturnal song.

When he tried to embrace her, she stepped back, as she had already done in the past. For a moment, he controlled himself, overwhelmed by doubts that had slipped into his mind when he thought of the sick baby who lived near the lake.

"Come on," he thought. "These fears are odious and ridiculous…"

He approached her again and this time she allowed him to embrace her as she trembled.

"Why are you trembling?" he asked gently.

She did not reply. She continued to tremble but made no effort to free herself. Mario saw a tear well up at the corner of her eye.

"What's wrong?" he asked her "Are my advances so painful for you?"

She turned her head away and burst into sobs. Upset, Mario moved away from her. He recalled the strange way she had behaved earlier, the precarious balance of her mind. An amnesiac? A story-teller? She was certainly easily terrified. Perhaps she was just subject to the already violent and chaotic hypersensitivity of very young girls? There was nothing surprising about her bursting into tears under such circumstances...

He moved closer and she accepted his embrace. From that moment, as if something had been definitely and permanently set into motion, she abandoned herself to him with a sort of fury through which Mario lost almost all notion of anything.

As they were lying side by side, body and mind pleasantly exhausted, two shots rang out in the distance.

CHAPTER XIII

Mario drove away his drowsiness and leapt for the window. The sky was red. Feverishly arranging his rumpled clothing, he embraced Francesca, who clung to him.

"No!" she shouted. "Don't go out! You don't know what's going on here! I don't want to see you in danger…"

Mario was struck by this attitude, which was similar to that of Benedetto and Angelina a few hours earlier and remained still for a moment, shivering. But he regained his self-control quickly and freed himself. He ran down the hallway, followed by Francesca's sobs.

Outside, the sinister ringing of the alarm pummeled his ears. He raced toward the village, where lights were turning on one by one. A glance in the direction of the mountains revealed the source of the light that had turned the sky blood red. Up above, on the slope of Monte Peccatore, Benedetto's farm was blazing.

"Madona!" he exclaimed in a heavy voice. "An accident, or… or an attack?"

He changed direction and rushed toward the now familiar path. Behind him, in the village, her heard voices shouting, doors slamming and the sound of heavy shoes hitting the hard soil. He paid no attention to the noise, focusing instead on avoiding the thorny branches as he raced on.

Soon, he reached the farm, without encountering anyone on his way. The blaze was immense. Flames sizzled as they fell to the ground, still damp from the recent rain.

"Madona!" he repeated.

He did not usually call on the Virgin for help. But the events had created a bond between him and the old man and his daughter stronger than if he had known and liked them for years...

He walked ahead, but the terrible heat of the fire forced him to retreat. He walked around the burning building and the barn, looking for solitary silhouettes in the vegetation that was violently illuminated by the flames.

But there was no one in the area.

"They can't be inside!" he thought, filled with horror.

He listened carefully but heard no one crying out or calling from the fire. Just as he returned to his starting point, he noticed a dark shape lying not far from the threshold to the building. Holding his arms across his face to protect it from the heat, he took a few steps ahead.

The body of a dog. Others lay on the ground, here and there.

"The dogs..." said Mario, as his blood ran cold. "All... all the dogs are dead. They killed them."

He shouted, "Benedetto! Angelina! Angelina!"

He thought he heard a faint moan in a thicket. His eyes widened in horror. In the middle of the dogs lay something he had initially assumed was a log: it was the body of a decapitated man. The head had rolled a few meters away. Benedetto's teeth shone, in the reflection of the flames, in a mouth twisted open in a last cry for help.

Trembling, Mario headed in the direction of the thicket from which the moan had come. On the side of the mountain, the sound of pounding feet and breaking branches announced the arrival of a large crowd, carrying flashlights to light their way. He bent down toward a bush and pulled out Angelina. She was only partially dressed and her eyes gleamed madly.

Shouting, men armed with pitchforks and guns scrambled up the slope. They surged into the light of the fire just as Mario, his face twisted in anguish walked toward them, carrying Angelina in his arms.

"Him again!" shouted a peasant. "He's the one who set the fire!"

"Idiot!" shouted a man in disheveled clothing, who took a place in front of the others. "Shut up! I know him and he's not responsible."

He turned to face them and said, "Quite the contrary. He's the first one to come to help Benedetto and his daughter while you wasted time building up your courage."

Dr. Casciattelli's imposing voice forced the peasants into silence. Mario walked toward him and placed a sobbing Angelina at his feet.

"She's injured..." he said in a toneless voice.

He turned his head away and added, "Her father... has been murdered."

Silence fell over the crowd. The dancing lights of the flames ran over the faces, hiding motionless grimaces.

Murdered!" someone said. "Those bastards! They'll pay for this!"

A voice sniggered, "Pay? How? What if it's them from the lake?"

Everyone shivered in horror. Some made the sign of the cross.

"Look..." said Mario pointing at the courtyard where a few pickets of the broken fence still stood. The gate had been destroyed.

Four men walked over, protecting their faces. When they caught sight of the decapitated cadaver, they crossed themselves again and retreated hastily.

The doctor, who was examining Angelina, stood up and called out, "Salgari!"

Mario turned to look at the man.

"Don't worry," said Casciattelli. "She's not injured. I think she's just had a nervous shock and should recover quickly."

"Thank you, doctor..." said Mario, somberly. "Her father was a brave man... Do you have any idea about what's happened?"

The man searched through his pocket, pulled out a handkerchief and wiped his forehead.

Then he said, "No... I was sleeping. Were you sleeping?"

Then it was Mario's turn to assume a blank expression.

"Yes," he said, his throat dry. "I was sleeping."

The doctor spread his arms, palms up, and tipped his asymmetrical head to one side.

"So, we're reduced to conjuring up conjectures... A thief no doubt... or several. No doubt, you know that this region is not well serviced by the police."

"Yes..." said Mario who did not believe a word. "And what do you think about what the peasants said? They mentioned 'them from the lake'."

The doctor shrugged without replying.

"Oh! Mario!" Angelina moaned weakly.

"Would you take care of her?" asked Mario. "I'd like to help the men take Benedetto back to the village. He was an excellent host to me and I quite liked him."

"Mario! No, don't leave me!" shouted Angelina sitting up. "No one can go to my father yet."

Sobs smothered her words.

"I'll... I'll tell you what happened. Only you."

Mario looked at her and felt his heart pounding.

"Wait a minute... just a minute..." he said, gently.

He headed in the direction of the fence, took a step beyond it and leapt back quickly, crying out. A shard of burning wood had just hit him in the face. He pushed it quickly away. His eyes widened in surprise and he rubbed his cheek, which had been singed by the projectile, with the back of his hand.

"I didn't... I didn't feel the burn!" he shouted, sounding dumbfounded.

The doctor took a step toward him.

"What?" he asked.

Mario looked at the other man and thought he looked distressed.

"I'll say it again," he said. "I didn't feel the burn."

Looking powerless, Casciattelli shrugged. Despite the red glow cast over everyone's faces, Mario thought he saw the man turn extremely pale. The doctor returned immediately to the peasants.

"Two of you stay nearby to watch over the body," he said. "We'll come back to get it morning the morning when it will be possible to get closer."

He turned away without another word and walked off through the pine trees.

Perplexed, Mario watched the man's silhouette dissolve in the shadows, which were growing thicker with the approach of dawn.

He went to sit near Angelina on the ground. His mind focused on the terrible foreboding dream he had had earlier at the now destroyed farm.

CHAPTER XIV

In snippets constantly interrupted by weeping, Angelina told Mario about the tragic events that had taken place on the farm after the journalist had left, pursuing the mysterious voice through the shadows.

Benedetto had gone out after Mario, but the younger man had raced off, as if irresistibly drawn by a force that overwhelmed him. The old man, limping with his wooden leg, had turned back and gone to join Angelina who was waiting on the doorstep, shivering. They both went inside and closed the door, although they kept vigil through a partly open window.

They spent a quarter of an hour like that then Angelina returned to her room. Benedetto continued his watch.

In her bed, Angelina was unable to sleep. Her room was at the back of the building and the young girl was able to spy over the night through her window. It was hot but, from time to time, a breath of cool air, a precursor of yet another storm, blew over the mountains. Since Angelina's room was on the ground floor it was easy to see what the moonlight drew out from the shadows.

At the same time, a vigilant ear would hear even the slightest sound. Overwhelmed by a growing apprehension, Angelina found sleep harder and harder to catch as time passed.

Almost an hour after Mario's departure, she thought she heard suspicious rustling sounds in the bushes. She got up without making a sound and silently closed her window. As she thought of the fate Mario had saved her from that very evening, the most disturbing fears filled her mind.

As she stood there, frozen, between her bed and the window, the door to her room opened suddenly.

Holding a gun, her father stood in the doorway, lit from behind by the light in the common room.

"Ah, you're up," he said.

He looked at her, then continued "Don't come out of your room. Promise that you won't come out, even if you hear something that frightens you."

She promised after her father insisted.

"Don't go out unless you're in danger here," he added.

And he closed the door.

For Angelina, that started a trial which seemed endless. She did not feel brave enough to expose herself to the potential danger, but she did not want to remain in the dark about what was threatening the farm, since her father obviously feared some sort of attack. She opened the window part way.

Just then, she heard trampling and panting that froze her blood. The evil ones were surrounding them.

Soon, the signs of their presence behind the buildings gradually disappeared. The dogs, which had been strangely silent up to that point, started howling, making an enormous racket at the front of the house.

A few seconds later, someone pounded at the door. Benedetto reappeared, looking both terrified and resolved.

"See if there's anyone behind the house..." he said to Angelina. "If those damned creatures get in, run!"

She did not have time to hug him... He headed back into the common room. Soon the door gave way.

"I'll get them anyway," Benedetto shouted.

Angelina heard the sound of a window opening, followed by two shots. He must have climbed through the window into the yard, despite his disability, shooting.

Angelina in turn climbed through the window and raced for the bushes. She started racing through the scrub then the light from the fire stopped her and she turned back cautiously. A flash of lightning in the distance zigzagged through the clouds, followed by a weak rumble.

When she was in sight of the buildings, there were no shapes dancing in front of the flames. The threatening storm had driven the creatures off. Angelina had walked around the farm, thinking that the attackers had used the cinders from the hearth to start the fire. As she watched it from a distance, she fainted in the bushes where Mario had found her.

Morning dawned. Hypnotized by the smoking embers from which small flames continued to rise, Mario sympathized deeply with Angelina's drama and tried to console her with empty words.

They sat together for a long time while the two peasants the doctor had assigned to watch over the body observed them discreetly.

Soon, they heard footsteps climbing up the slope. Angelina sat up straight and cried out in fright.

"No, "Mario said gently. "They're from the village..."

The crowd approached. The people at the front were carrying a stretcher. Angelina looked back and almost fainted again when the men placed Benedetto's remains on the stretcher. They covered the body with an old brown blanket and prepared to leave while other peasants approached Angelina, offering her their condolences.

Just then Mario caught sight of Francesca.

Angelina had joined the funeral group and, her eyes brimming with tears, she had barely noticed Francesca's presence. Mario walked over to the doctor's niece. He was extremely troubled and Francesca's attitude did nothing to calm him. She lowered her head, avoided Mario's eyes, and turned away to avoid seeing the ruins. Yet, she was the first to speak.

"I... I was afraid that something had happened to you..." she said.

He studied her with a complex feeling of curiosity and mistrust, all the while wanting to hold her in his arms.

"No," he said. "I have no idea why you would have such fears... Perhaps you know more than I do about the sinister phenomena that have been taking place here?"

She grimaced.

"No..." she said quickly. "You know full well that I've only been in Santa Croce three days..."

Mario snorted, then said, "I've only been here thirty-six hours and I've seen a ton of abnormal things, including this despicable murder and this fire..."

He looked her up and down, then added, "Those abnormal things include... your so-called amnesia... and your fear of the storm... And also the strange resemblance between your voice and the one I heard at the top of the dam..."

She placed her arms around his neck.

"No," he said. "I do admit that I love you, but that's no reason for such displays..."

He stopped talking and embraced her violently. Yet, just a few seconds later, he returned to the thread of his furious observations. Questions forced their way to his lips.

"Did you know that the child who lives near the lake is ill?"

She turned pale but remained silent.

After a few seconds, she replied, "No I didn't know that."

Mario continued to study her. Hypotheses swirled about in his mind, but they all seemed so ridiculous he rejected them almost immediately.

Francesca glanced quickly around.

"We must part," she said suddenly. "My uncle... went out earlier. I must not get back too long after him."

Abruptly, she took two steps back, looked at him with an expression of deep sadness, then walked lightly through the bushes. She disappeared in the blink of an eye.

Mario stood there, undecided and furious. Obviously, she had used that pretext to avoid answering questions she considered embarrassing and dangerous.

In flash, Marios was suddenly certain of one thing Mario: Francesca was not Dr. Casciattelli's niece. And from there, it took just one small step to think that she was in cahoots with those who were haunting the night, spreading an unknown disease and killing isolated farmers.

But Mario was too filled with disgust to take that step, fearing that it would bring other suppositions.

He headed back in the direction of the village, feeling as if his head were caught in a vice.

On his way, he decided to stop in at the doctor's house and ask the man for the explanations he had refused to give him. If Francesca were present, all the better.

CHAPTER XV

She had lied again. When Mario went to see Dr. Casciattelli, there was no trace of Francesca, although she had said she was going back there. When he saw the young man, the doctor nodded, his brow furrowed.

"Other symptoms?" he asked.

This time, it was Mario's turn to frown.

"What do you mean, by other symptoms?"

The doctor suddenly seemed uncomfortable.

"Oh," he said. "I just asked you that out of professional politeness."

Mario observed the other man, suspicious. He no longer trusted anyone. Yet he had only one thought in his mind.

"Frances... Miss Francesca isn't here?" he asked.

Casciattelli stiffened strangely.

"No..." he said. "Do you... do you know her?"

"A bit," said Mario. "We met."

The doctor let him in. He looked concerned.

"So," he said. "You've met Francesca..."

He stumbled over his words. Suddenly, he turned toward his visitor and looked at him darkly.

"Oh," he said. "What's with all this dissimulation? You should know that Francesca is not my niece contrary to her claims."

Mario smiled tightly.

"I wondered," he said.

Casciattelli shrugged.

"Don't smile," he said abruptly. "This morning my mind is relatively clear and all this nonsense is stifling me."

Mario felt that the other man was about to clarify a few aspects of the problem he was circling about.

"Yes?" he said to encourage the doctor.

"Sit down," said the other man. "What I have to tell you is very delicate. I have very bad news for you!"

Mario sat down in a comfortable chair in the office. This was the third room he had entered in the house and the furniture was no less strange, no less luxurious than in the others. Casciattelli had clasped his hands and was staring at the carpet.

"Mr. Salgari," he said. "You are seriously ill."

Mario shivered unpleasantly. Without admitting it, he had been expecting that...

"You must be brave," continued the doctor. "The disease... the disease is *leprosy*."

The journalist felt dizzy. Leprosy! That nightmare disease... In a flash, he recalled his dream. It was continuing.

"How... how do you know that?" he stammered, terrified.

Casciattelli shrugged.

"That's easy," he said, suddenly weary. "I know that you spent half the night in my home, with Francesca... What's the point of hiding that? Francesca is a leper. Well... to the extent that she exists..."

Mario was finding it hard to follow what the doctor was saying. He had the man repeat his last words.

"Yes," said the doctor. I can't stop now that I've started. I must tell you everything I know... or everything I think I know."

He stopped a moment to collect his thoughts, then continued.

"Almost two years ago, I came here on vacation, to take in some harpoon fishing. My main office is in Rome. I wanted to see if I could find nice specimens in a lake, specimens as nice as those in the sea."

He settled back, leaned his head against the back of the chair and stared at Mario through half-closed eyes.

"I would have been better off attaching an anchor around my neck..." he said. "I'm sure you know that the reservoir is not very deep. Along with the air tanks and the excellent mask I wore to fly among the houses of the old village, I also carried a special flashlight that revealed such an extraordinary world to me I forgot all about fishing. Imagine a drowned village!"

"I can picture it," said Mario.

He thought of the sinister creatures that had dived into the lake after he had torn Angelina from their claws. He also thought of Francesca's unsettling song, rising *through the water...*

"Like any other village, it had a church. As far as I could see, using the sunlight that flowed through the water and my flashlight, the church in the lake was still in good condition. Believe me... it was extremely strange to see fish swimming in and out through walls once filled with stained-glass windows, the very same windows that were moved to the new church and broken recently."

He paused.

"I decided to go into the church," he continued. "My second bad decision. That's when the nightmare started."

"The nightmare?"

"What else can it be called? Despite what I have to tell you, don't think that I'm terribly open to the supernatural. Generally, I believe what I can see and that's it. Well, let me tell you that I can't believe what I saw that day. And it all holds together so well and has now reached such a peak that I keep coming up with a host of explanations that convince me that the entire village, myself included... that we are all suffering from madness. Because, if we are all of sound mind... all we would have to do is destroy everything that lies behind our reasoning and blindly believe just about anything."

"Get to the facts of the matter!" said Mario, impatiently.

Mario was eager for the doctor to conclude his account so he could ask about his own case. In fact, he was only listening with half an ear so great was his terror over his condition.

"I'm getting to it... I'm getting to it..." said Casciattelli. "I swam up to one of the openings. I followed the fish. The stone vault that formed the roof of the nave had withstood the pressure of the water—which was the same both inside and outside the church. But little light entered the building and I had to rely on my flashlight."

He sighed, then continued, "The interior surface of the walls had been designed with alcoves containing stone benches. All of the benches were occupied."

"Cadavers?" asked Mario.

Casciattelli stared at him.

"No," he said. "But not exactly living beings, either."

Mario shrugged, although he had a clear idea of where the other man was heading.

"What then? What is neither living nor dead?"

"Those I saw that day and who torched Benedetto's farm this night."

"And you, a man of science, dare to say such things to me?" asked Mario, without placing too much emphasis on his words.

"Yes," said the doctor, with restrained fury. "And if I'm mad, so is the entire village. You probably are too if you've seen anything at all here and if you believed your eyes."

Mario looked down.

"In the alcoves…" said Casciattelli, "In the alcoves, I saw creatures wearing gray robes and hoods that floated around their bodies as they moved. And they were moving."

"You were hallucinating."

"That's what I immediately thought. But when I wanted to leave the same way I came in, for some well needed rest, one of those impossible creatures stood in my way and ordered me, with a gesture, to remain where I was."

"It's hard to remain still in the water," commented Mario, mocking the other man.

"Joke if you will," said the doctor. "But wait to hear the rest. By some sort of telepathic means, I realized that these creatures were forbidding me to reveal their existence to those on the surface. And I recall that, at that time, I amused myself for a few seconds conversing mentally with my hallucination. I told them to rest assured, that I wouldn't say a word to anyone in the village, much less to people in Rome… with the exception of a psychiatrist colleague, perhaps."

Casciattelli shrugged then continued, "Just then, the light from my flashlight danced like lightning through the water. The creature that had blocked my way was holding some sort of ancient dagger. He brandished it over my head and I felt a blinding pain in my left ear. Blood clouded the water in front of me. I swam ahead, toward the opening, rejecting the apparition. Not quickly enough, though, to avoid hearing this thought from outside my head: 'We're taking this as a pledge of your silence. We will use it to hold you to your word.' I returned to the surface using my hand to stem the bleeding as I quickly lost strength."

"How did you account for your injury?" asked Mario. "I mean, how did you seriously explain it?"

"I managed to get home, where I prepared a make-do bandage. Then I headed to Rome the very same day. I took drugs so I would be able to drive. Over the following weeks I gradually convinced myself that I had caught my ear on the frame of the stain-glass window. However, one image stuck with me: the hand I thought I saw holding a dagger. Two fingers were missing from that hand. It could be a result of gangrene or leprosy."

He leaned toward Mario and said, "Since then, I've learned that there was once an asylum not far from the drowned village. It was there until the 17th century I believe."

His thoughts whirling about, Mario recalled the impossible excursion Francesca had told him about, her trip to the Venetto abbey...

"And Francesca da Ricci?" he said, with an effort.

"Ah, her... She's one of those... part our collective hallucination, the hallucination that kills some people, contaminates others and sets fires. She was sent to the surface to provide a link to this century. She told me herself that she came from a noble family that once owned the entire region up to Naples. Bohemians had brought leprosy here in 1550 and Francesca lived from 1608 to

1625. She committed suicide at the age of 17 after contact with a leprous servant, to avoid seeing the disease ravage her body month after month."

Mario jerked back violently. Dr. Casciattelli had lost his mind. He was stark raving mad and was doing everything he could to share his mental illness with others.

"Do you realize what you're saying?" he asked.

"I most certainly do," replied Casciattelli. "Now, let's get back to your case."

"Listen, doctor," said Mario. "I prefer to consult one of your colleagues."

Casciattelli looked at him curiously.

"You seem to think it's normal that you didn't feel any pain when the ember hit your cheek..." he observed calmly. "Believe you me, that's not normal. Lack of sensation occurs at the neurological stage of the infection. This form of leprosy is extremely virulent and becomes generalized immediately after contamination, following a single contact, unlike the usual variant of the disease."

He shrugged.

"Perhaps in the case of skin cuts, no bacteria would be found... perhaps those who are infected are suffering from some sort of *psychotic leprosy...* with functional, subjective symptoms..."

He appeared quite clear as he looked at Mario.

"But in that case why had the child I went to see at the lake lost two toes on his right foot?"

"And Francesca?" shouted Mario, losing control and struggling to fight his terror. "Was Francesca missing a leg?"

"She committed suicide shortly after contact with the leper. The disease remained in the early stage and there was no sign of it. That did not prevent her from contaminating you."

"What is this nonsense about germs that have been dead for three centuries coming to us through ghosts?" screamed Mario. "How can you expect me to believe a story like that?"

Dr. Casciattelli stood up.

"Don't think about the causes, think about the effects," he said coldly. "Now I would like you to leave me alone."

Mario tried to control himself.

"Seriously, doctor," he said. "Do you have any idea what is actually going on?"

Casciattelli remained standing and watched him for a moment then said, "We have several elements that seem to react with one another. First: the lepers do exist in some manner. There's no need to go crazy about the details, such as their noisy panting. I presume you've heard that. That's part of the appearance they've taken on, part of what makes them what they are. There's no point in wondering how they can stay under water. They're not really living... They're always the same whether they're under water or on land."

Mario waited patiently.

"And what about their deep nature?"

Casciattelli shrugged.

"Everything around us, our very selves, and all matter in general.... None of this exists in the form which senses reveal to us. It's all a matter of various arrangements of force fields. I'm sure you know that modern physics has clearly demonstrated the inexistence of matter... What we take for a defined object is just the result of a mental operation, based on sensory images that we form of it.

"Such a forcefield will create the impression of a color through our retina, which serves as a translating machine... of mass through other such translating machines operated by the tactile particles of our skin... and so on."

"I know," said Mario. "But where are you going with this?"

"On to the next idea. All in all, the universe is merely a whirlpool of moving forces, an immense network of waves. These waves include those emitted by the human brain—electroencephalograms have proven this. Up to now, we've found no traces of brain waves emitted in the past by those who lived before us, perhaps because such waves were too weak. But, let us consider two human settlements located close to one another: a village that is frequently struck by destiny and an asylum. Such an asylum, like any other place where there are sick people, and particularly lepers, as in the case at hand, brings together an abnormal amount of suffering. Are you following me?"

"Yes," said Mario, frowning.

"So, we have two sites with an abnormal emotional potential. Now, let's suppose that the brain waves of those who lived there over the years modified, in some manner or another and as subtly as possible, the sites in question. Suddenly, the asylum is destroyed, releasing this potential, which is concentrated on the remaining site, doubling the intensity of that site's potential."

"Hm," said Mario, grimacing. "I see where this is taking us."

"The progressive release of that accumulated force, resulted in abnormal phenomena. And, I would like to point out, such phenomena have nothing to do with what our senses tell us. They result in destruction. Let's just say that our minds, which are accustomed to translating everything we learn into a concrete material form, restore those that left their mark on the places where they once lived in their primitive appearance."

"That's ingenuous," said Mario, thoughtfully. "With a little bit of rationalization, your interpretation is quite similar to the simple thoughts good old Benedetto explained to me..."

The doctor sat back down and concluded, "Simple people have a sort of intuition. I believe that, given their superstitious natures, everyone in the village has a similar view of the matter. I merely speak for them all, starting with the notion of minerals that gather emotions and connecting it all to the current state of our scientific knowledge."

"But how can we fight that?" asked Mario, fearing that he was losing his mind.

Casciattelli stared at him.

"I'm involved in the situation," he said lucidly. "I've been involved since I dove into that lake where an exceptional combination of circumstances created an exceptional energy. I'm caught up in the gears. If we destroy the machine, I will disappear with it."

Mario was silent.

"However, I do believe we have to blow up the dam," added the doctor.

Mario remained silent for a moment, then shrugged and said, "Supposing that's a solution.... You can't demolish such a mass with a hunting rifle."

The doctor smiled briefly, and said, "I've been thinking about this for a year. I've been able to obtain some plastic explosives, using shady means, from a warehouse the American army abandoned ten years ago. I have everything we need, detonators and all that..."

He thought for a moment, then added, "It will require sabotage... can you see us presenting our plan to the authorities... giving them the arguments you now know? Such an extreme undertaking will have to be a purely individual effort... and it will most likely be considered insane. But what do we know about what is being planned? Where will this invasion stop and how? And, above all, what type of epidemic is threatening the country?"

He slapped his forehead and said, "Anyway, no matter how serious your case is, I think you should start treatment immediately. Please note that I fear it might be completely useless... but we still have to try."

Mario watched as the other man stood up and looked through a medicine cabinet filled with boxes of all shapes and colors.

"A simple shot..." said Casciattelli.

Worried, Mario wondered what he should say to that. What was worse? An unlikely disease but one that would be terrifying if he had been infected? Or some unbelievable treatment? Unless Casciattelli was right?

"What's that?" he asked.

The doctor broke the tip off a glass vial and filled a syringe with liquid.

"Streptomycin," he replied tersely.

Casciattelli's serious air filled Marios with horror. What if he *really* did have leprosy?

Voice hoarse, he asked "Is... Is streptomycin... effective?"

The doctor grimaced and, in an ominous voice, said "In the case of let us say, normal patients, we get good results. It is combined with sulfones and Chaulmoogra oil... But this strain of leprosy has never been seen before. In principle, you need to be in contact with lepers over a period of several years in order to be contaminated and the incubation period lasts from three months to three years. The lesions develop very slowly. In your case and even more so in the case of the infant, I feel like I'm seeing a caricature of the disease... and the progression of the illness has accelerated at an insane pace."

"In any case, get to Rome as quickly as you can for treatment."

Sweat beading on his forehead, Mario, accepted the injection.

CHAPTER XVI

Mario's mind was so confused when he left the doctor that he could not think clearly. As he walked, he thought about the last words Casciattelli had spoken to him.

"I can't believe this is Hansen's disease. Get yourself tested and give the lab results to the specialist you see. I believe this type of leprosy can be treated better with electric shock therapy than anything else... It is the mind that is affected by this sort of infection."

He accompanied Mario out onto the front porch, then added, "Unless bacteria were created at the same time as human beings... No matter which way you look at the problem, it is not an easy one to solve. We are up to our necks in a living nightmare..."

These words did nothing at all to comfort Mario, who was seriously starting to think he was going mad.

Hammer blows rang out through the village in a sinister manner.

"The carpenter is nailing Benedetto's coffin," thought Mario, with a grimace. "When will it be my turn?"

Most of the people of Santa Croce had gathered in the church. The shattered stained-glass from the windows had been swept up and piled near the door.

Mario walked over to it and glanced into the nave. It was filled with men and women, all whispering animatedly. In the middle of the nave, not far from the alter, four candles burned around an improvised gurney that had been placed on the large tiles. Benedetto's body waited there, hidden by the same brown blanket as the previous night. Kneeling nearby, Angelina was weeping, attended by several women who obviously shared her pain.

"Mr. Salgari!" someone shouted.

Mario turned his head and saw who was calling him. It was the innkeeper. She was standing inside the church, a few meters from the entrance.

"Yes," he said, stepping into the nave.

"You have to pay your bill..." the woman said. "I'm closing today."

He looked at her indifferently and said, "Whatever..."

She rolled her eyes.

"Not here..." she finally said. "Later, after the funeral service."

This caught Mario's attention briefly.

"The priest is coming today?"

"Yes. He should be here any minute now."

Mario glanced through the open door, for a moment, at the dirt track that ran from the church to the small road. Then he looked back at the inert body.

"Poor Angelina..." he said, sadly.

"Of course," said the innkeeper. "But if this continues..."

The sound of a car motor rose from the road.

The villagers quickly went outside onto the church steps where the noon day sun turned the stones a blinding yellow. Behind the low wall of the small cemetery next to the church, medals and glass miniatures hung from the arms of the cross like small suns. Likenesses of the Virgin Mary were everywhere to be seen. Mario felt

236

Angelina's talisman in his pocket... but did those naïve objects have any power to chase away the shadow? Mario made a discreet sign of the cross as he watched two cars drive ahead.

The innkeeper, who was still at his side, said "Ah yes. Giuseppe, the mayor's son, biked to Mammola this morning to notify the police. It won't do much good, but a man did die, so..."

The first car, a Jeep, carried four men in uniform armed with machine guns. Mario found the scene almost laughable. The presence of such weapons was so ridiculous!

Behind the Jeep, the priest's small Fiat quickly climbed the slope. The two cars came to a stop, one behind the other, at the entrance to the church. They were immediately surrounded by people shouting and waving their arms. The police jumped down from the Jeep, pushing the villagers back. The door of the Fiat opened and Mario saw a corpulent priest, carrying his round hat in his hand, step out.

"Padre! Padre!" shouted several women.

They seemed to be on the verge of hysteria. The priest noticed this and immediately took them into the church on the heels of three uniformed police officers and the mayor, a weary looking, silent man. The fourth police officer remained outside watching over the weapons the three others had left behind before going into the church.

One of the officers came back out and looked around the crowd.

"Mr. Salgari!" he shouted. "Where is Mr. Salgari?"

Mario walked over to the man, irritated. Naturally, he would not avoid the interrogation. He was the last one to see Benedetto alive. Were they going to ask him for an alibi? How could he admit that he had spent the night with Francesca?

But the interrogation was over soon. Mario had already been cleared by Angelina.

As he walked away from the police officer, another man in uniform stepped out of the church and quietly said, "Everyone in Santa Croce has gone crazy..."

The police headed back out along the yellow road with their weapons. They were going to investigate the fire at the farm, then visit Dr. Casciattelli to get a death certificate.

The doctor had performed a quick autopsy early that morning to confirm that Benedetto had been killed with an axe and that the decapitation had occurred after the victim was already dead. It was just a formality since there had been a crime...

Mario watched them drive off, then went into the church to attend the funeral service.

The carpenter brought the coffin in at the beginning of the mass and the service was delayed so that Benedetto could be placed in the plain wooden box after being hastily sewn into a sheet scented with thyme and lavender.

Angelina stood to the side. In the midst of the women, she seemed absent, alone, barely conscious. The other villagers were starting to lose interest since the priest had not adequately assessed the scope of the evil that had struck Santa Croce and his sermon was far too violent. He used the terror he saw on the faces of the members of his flock to enhance his oratorical efforts and depict the gates of hell gaping under the feet of the sinners. It was the last thing he should have done since it threw three-quarters of the churchgoers into a panic.

Feeling an urgent need after the mass, the priest led a procession that slowly made its way to the dam.

Mario had not left the church and he took part in the procession, carrying a candle. He had not grown any more devout over the past 24 hours but, since his vision of the world had crumbled dangerously, he tried to drum up some courage by duping himself and imitating the gestures of those who placed themselves under the protection of God.

Along the way, he recalled Dr. Casciattelli's opinions: all in all, could this procession serve as a collective electric shock?

As they approached the dam, a woman raced out of one of the huts and threw herself to her knees in front of the priest, holding the child she carried in her arms up to him. Mario recognized the woman he had met the first night, the one who had sent him to see Benedetto. So, the child... He turned away. Selfishness took over and he thought about his own situation as the priest shook an aspergillum over the baby.

This was followed by an exorcism ceremony. The priest placed candles on the parapet and addressed Satan in Latin. His faithful followers chanted the prayer after him and he then threw holy water into the reservoir. Leaning over the parapet, Mario, saw something strange just then: many, many bubbles were floating to the surface at several spots on the calm water, breaking there. Then the water grew still once more and reflected the sky that had been almost clear since the morning.

People cried out, beseeching God. The women walked from one end of the dam to the other on their knees and the men stood there, frozen, arms crossed, murmuring prayers. Mario felt that the priest seemed irritated as he called the villagers back to order. He seemed to find something ridiculous about exorcising a mass of concrete built to generate electricity and the artificial lake held behind it. He had not believed what he had been told...

Somehow, the villagers got back into line and headed off to the village, singing hymns. As they reached the first houses, silence fell over them. A worried silence. Soon, the villagers broke away from the procession and the priest found himself alone with Mario and Angelina. Someone had drawn large crosses on the doors of the houses in white chalk. Horrified, the villagers felt that God had abandoned them. They opened their doors, taking care not to touch the chalk marks. Inside each house, the villagers gave into an unusual frenzy of cleaning.

CHAPTER XVII

Panic, which had been threatening since the discovery and transportation of Benedetto's body, was taking hold of Santa Croce in a single wave. Already, carts were being pulled out of sheds, coupled to donkeys and loaded to the brim. The same tense, impatient expressions could be found on all faces and those who had initially decided to stay behind in the village were now frightened at the thought of remaining there along, at the mercy of disgusting creatures, and more vulnerable than ever, isolated among deserted house.

No cries, no shouts. Only the silent and feverish activity of people tearing themselves away from the land where they had always lived because fear had been victorious. Many tears, once held back, started flowing painfully over fierce faces. Isolated like a shipwreck on the waves, Mario, wandered among the villagers as they prepared for their exile.

Initially, when the police returned from the expedition, they had tried, with the priest's support, to stem this terrified flood. They had begged, beseeched, threatened, all in vain.

Those they had managed to convince to change their minds, making them believe that it was a good idea to stay behind and not abandon what made up their very fiber, changed their minds again, throwing themselves back into their primitive resolution. The sound of hooves and wheels filled the fear-swept village.

Mario had paid his bill at the inn. Obviously, the innkeeper and her neighbors were leaving with the hope of being able to return... those who had resolved to abandon almost everything they owned closed their doors carefully, with the obvious intention of returning once the horror had dissipated.

The first few carts set out in the direction of Mammola. Drawn together by common interest, other families formed tribes to emigrate to Olmeto.

As time passed, the village slowly lost the sinister frenzy of activity that often follows major catastrophes: wars, epidemics, famines. Mario thought about his discussions with Benedetto and the doctor: Santa Croce was re-experiencing, through some hideous fatality, the pains and disasters that had afflicted the old village. And, as if the sky had played a role in the defeat, the clouds were returning in black battalions over the mountain peaks, transforming the blinding light into a gray canopy where colors died.

"Signor... Salgari... I believe?" said a voice close to Mario.

The journalist spun about, as if he had been stung. It was only the priest, his slumped shoulders and defeated expression revealing both surprise and consternation.

"Yes, padre?" asked Mario.

"You... You aren't leaving?" the priest asked hesitantly.

He turned to look at the carts.

"You aren't being driven away by the devil, like the others?"

"I don't believe in the devil," answered Mario. "And I have an investigation that I can't interrupt."

He glanced at the inn with its shuttered windows.

"For that matter, my Lambretta is out of commission and, over the past 48 hours, I've had to spend my time on something other than its repairs. As I had initially intended."

The priest was watching him curiously.

"What exactly do you know about what is going on here?" he asked, sounding embarrassed.

Mario smiled glumly.

"I believe I know a lot of things, but I don't think any of them are exact," he replied. "And since my camera stayed behind at the farm, it was destroyed by the fire... that's too bad since there was one shot..."

He rubbed his hand across his cheek, where the burning ember had touched him and added, "I would very much like for this entire, enormous mystery to be explained. Unfortunately, I do believe that uncontrollable, evil forces have been released in this region and your ministry will be as powerless before them as machine guns."

The priest continued to study him.

"That's basically what the mayor told he and I criticized him for not having more faith in divine Providence..." he said, sounding regretful.

"This village may have been under the care of Providence... but that was in the past," said Mario. "Since that time, it has changed hands and I'm not certain the villagers are wrong to abandon it."

While talking, they had walked back to the church and gone into it. In the coffin, Benedetto's body was still waiting for burial. A few meters from it, Angelina knelt on a kneeler, motionless. When they approached her, they found her plunged in a stupor.

The sound of footsteps made them both turn back. Dr. Casciattelli was entering the nave.

"So, it's a defeat…"

He noticed Angelina, who had not turned about at the sound of his voice and abandoned the fake, glib tone he had adopted.

Walking over to the priest, he murmured "You have no men to bury this poor man. Will you accept my help?"

He looked at Mario, and asked "Will you join us Salgari?"

It was not easy for the three men to carry the coffin on their own. And their efforts were hampered by the fact that Angelina had roused from her torpor and burst into sobs, begging them to delay the hasty burial.

But the three men stood firm and managed to keep Angelina inside the church as they carried the body into the small cemetery. Once there, the doctor found the gravedigger's tools at the back of a shed and they set to work.

A storm was threatening, as usual, but it did not burst and twilight invaded the village as they were pain-fully lowering the coffin into the grave. They shoveled the damp soil on top of the coffin and planted a wrought iron cross discovered along with the tools.

The wearied priest said good-bye to Mario and the doctor and went to give Angelina some comfort. But he came back out of the church almost immediately as the young girl had collapsed on the kneeler, falling into an exhausted sleep.

The police officers' Jeep had left the village much earlier. Now it was the Fiat's turn.

"Will you take care of Angelina?" Mario asked Casciattelli. "I have to check some things in my luggage, which the innkeeper placed near my Lambretta, in the shed…"

The physician stared at the journalist in the twilight.

"Of course," he said, rubbing his dirt covered hands. "I'll take her to my place. She'll be there when you… when you want to see her…"

Mario turned those words over in his mind, thanked the doctor abruptly, and strode off.

CHAPTER XVIII

After the doctor had stepped through the church door, Mario changed direction. He turned his back on the inn and started to run toward the dam, arriving there quickly.

Once there, he felt stupid... The evening dampness wrapped around his shoulders and, although the air was warm, he shivered. In the suspicious light that precedes night, the water held in place by the enormous concrete dam was as mysterious as the dam was powerfully majestic. The clouds moving swiftly across the sky and the bluish light that hid everything mingled with the scent of the juniper trees, the heavy odor of clay, the mineral silence, shrinking man while including him in nature. Mario felt lost, destroyed. The idea of calling Francesca—an idea that had come to him before he left the doctor, suddenly seemed ridiculous, grotesque, barbaric.

He headed slowly toward the shore, worried at the thought of suddenly finding himself face to face with a group of creatures. As he was about to step onto the concrete road that led to the dam, he heard something rustle behind him.

He whirled about. Two meters away, a hooded shape stood motionless. As he started to flee, a voice spoke.

"Mario," said the voice, muffled by fabric. "It's me... Francesca."

Mario stopped, took a few steps back. His heart was pounding, but not with fear. He moved closer and, with a hesitant gesture, pushed back the hood that hid the woman's face. the bluish light of twilight revealed Francesca's expression twisted with the pain of a violent inner combat.

"You should have left my face covered," she said in a weak voice. "We have to say farewell and the separation will be harder this way."

He took a step forward.

"Farewell?" he said. "Why? The village is abandoned but I'm staying."

He felt his words were moving faster than his thoughts, that through the young girl a monstrous universe was moving, one that was only human in appearance and that his knowledge of that universe was destroying the fragile bridge lies had built between them. Also, as he approached her, he felt both a painful love and a shapeless fear.

Wringing her hands, she waved Mario's protests away, saying, "I wanted to tell you that I did everything in my power to protect you last night. I called you before you left the old man, before the danger arrived. And yet you're sick, like I am, like we all are... that was another danger I exposed you to."

Her voice broke.

"But you would have learned everything from the doctor... you would have rejected me. I saw things like that. And now it's all been pointless since I am going to return to the void."

He cried out and took a step toward her.

"No, no..." she said. "I don't know where I'm coming from. I recall my life since drinking that poison. That day seems so close at hand! And I learned in this different village just how long ago it was in fact... By some chance, I was able to know the world of nights and days, the world of life, once again. Above all, I was given a chance to know you and I can now return to the shadows because, with you, I have re-experienced an existence that was interrupted far too early."

Mario moved so quickly she could not stop him. He took her in his arms and held her for a long time. His thoughts whirled about like terrified birds in his shattered mind and all he could do was repeat Francesca's name over and over again.

She finally tore herself from his embrace and stepped quickly away.

"Get away, now... It's night. In a moment, the dam that holds back the water will break into dust. The doctor has planned everything, prepared everything. From inside his house, the one where I received you, he will destroy the dam with a single stroke. The water will flow and all of us, all of us from the lake, we will return to the soil."

With a loud shout, Mario leapt ahead and grabbed her in his arms. Then he rushed down the road, his race made all the more difficult by Francesca's struggles to escape. Without slowing, he continued to murmur words in her ear, promising to stay by her side forever, to love her more and more with each passing day, telling her about where she came from, talking about the illness that affected both of them... telling her that she was as important to him as the air he breathed and saying that he would die with her if he could not stop the doctor's fatal action in time.

He arrived at the gate exhausted. He kicked it open violently and was racing toward the front porch when a gigantic explosion lit up the valley, its resounding echoes rolling from peak to peak. He turned around, horri-

fied at the thought that something irreparable had occurred. In his arms, Francesca felt as light as the wind.

The light came from the dam. The roar of rushing
water followed the last rumbles of thunder rejected by
the mountains.

Mario stood there, in the middle of the wild plants
in the garden, frozen. When he reached out his arms in a
desperate gesture to hug Francesca's body, they closed
on emptiness. With a moan, he fell forward, face down
on the damp ground.

When he regained consciousness, a terrible storm
was raging around him. The wind, a veritable hurricane,
was sweeping over the valley with a strident, continuous
screech, pushing plumes of warm water that drowned
everything in its path. Second after second, the deep
night was lit up by the red and purple flashes of lightning that struck the water of the lake relentlessly, connecting the sky and the earth. The immense roar of thunder mingled with the downpour falling over the pines
and the scrub bushes and the din of the water cascading
in the distance away from the sabotaged dam.

Mario got to his feet unsteadily and, guided by the
flashes of lightning, he headed automatically in the direction of the house, the walls standing out of the shadows, pale by moments, bloody by others, with each
flash.

Before climbing up the steps to the porch, he
glanced back at the drowned garden. Several flashes of
lightning revealed that there was no living being there.
This sudden solitude, following his mad dash holding
Francesca's body against his own, tore a moan from his
lips. He whirled about to face the door, which he shoved
open.

In the hall, a slender shaped cried out in fear when he entered, then ran back into the depths of the house. Dumbfounded, Mario took a few steps, then pushed another door open.

A violent light blinded him. he stepped into the parlor where the closed window was hidden by heavy, dark, velvet curtains. Dr. Casciattelli sat in an armchair facing him. His left hand was resting on a handle that rose up from a cubic box standing on the floor. Wires ran from it into the hall, the garden, the scrubland, the dam... he had set up everything during the course of the day. Perhaps he had spent several months procuring what he needed. A smile frozen on his face, the doctor stared at Mario without saying a word. Suddenly overwhelmed with fury, the young man approached the doctor and grabbed him by the lapels of his jacket.

The doctor slipped gently to the side. Mario took a step back, his heart pounding. He had noticed two things at the same time: the doctor was dead... and the left side of his head was intact.

Trembling, Mario walked out of the parlor and into the vestibule. There, he recalled the terrified silhouette he had seen on his way in. Other memories crowded into his mind.

The first thing he did was take his knife out of his pocket. A confused idea was germinating in his painful mind: he had to know if the disease was continuing to ravage his body. He clicked the blade open. Slowly, he lifted the tip of the blade to his face where the mark made by the burning ember could still be seen on his cheek. With a quick movement, he slashed his skin. He cried out immediately. He could feel again. This fake disease had certainly started to ravage his body, but it had also certainly been stopped by the doctor's initiative.

He thought about Dr. Casciattelli's sacrifice. Everything seemed to indicate that it had not been in vain. Francesca's intolerable disappearance would seem all the more final if Mario's illness had also returned to the world of shadows.

The thought of his restored health did little to comfort him, considering the suffering he was struggling against just then. He had to escape from that suffering one way or another.

He slowly closed his knife with trembling fingers and looked, wide-eyed, through the shadow.

"Angelina!" he shouted. "Angelina! It's me, Mario Salgari! Don't be afraid!"

He heard the sound of a door opening in the depths of the house. A weak, trembling voice called out through the darkness.

"It's ... Signor Mario?" she repeated.

Yes!" shrieked Mario, shivering with hope at the thought of leaving behind this terrible solitude, at the idea of experiencing a real presence, a living presence, and even better, someone weak, someone gentle, someone he had to protect... someone for whom he counted.

Angelina stepped into the light cast through the open door of the parlor. She was wearing the black coat over the white nightgown she had worn on the night of her father's tragic death.

Mario caught the young girl's expression. Her eyes were filled with admiration and trust. Fear and pain were retreating. His expression must have been similar. She squeaked in surprise and moved closer to him.

"Oh!" he said. "If you knew how much I need you."

As she heard those words, a new strength swelled up in her and she looked at him with dry, burning eyes.

He sighed deeply, as if holding back a sob.

"We'll set out for Naples, tomorrow," he said.
She wrapped her arms around him.